tears of a tiger

After a while the car started to sway, but I wasn't sure if it was me gettin' dizzy or if the car really was weaving across the expressway. At the time it seemed really funny. We was laughin' so hard—especially when people started honkin' at us. The more they tried to signal us, and I guess, warn us, the more we was crackin' up and laughin'. Rob had his feet up on the dashboard, partly actin' silly, and partly 'cause his legs was so long that they got cramped in that little car of Andy's. Me and B. J. was in the backseat. I was sittin' right behind Andy, and B. J. was sittin' next to me, behind Rob, 'cause he had the shortest legs, and Rob could push the seat all the way back.

Then, all of a sudden, like outta nowhere, this wall was in front of us, like it just jumped out in front of the car, and Andy was trying to find the brakes with his foot, and then there was glass everywhere and this crunchin', grindin' sound. My door flew open, and I rolled out. I remember I was cryin' and crawlin' around on my hands and knees—that's the only thing that got hurt on me—I got glass in my hands and in my knees.

tears of a tiger

sharon m. draper

Simon Pulse

The poem "One Thousand Nine Hundred and Sixty-eight Winters" by Jacqueline Earley appears here with the gracious permission of the author.

First paperback edition February 1996

Simon Pulse
An imprint of Simon & Schuster
Children's Publishing Division
1230 Avenue of the Americas
New York, NY 10020

Also available in an Atheneum Books for Young Readers hardcover edition.
Manufactured in the United States of America

40 39

The Library of Congress has cataloged the hardcover edition as follows:
Draper, Sharon M. (Sharon Mills)
Tears of a tiger / by Sharon M. Draper. — 1st ed.
p. cm.
Summary: The death of high school basketball star Rob Washington in an automobile accident affects the lives of his close friend Andy, who was driving the car, and many others in the school.
ISBN-13: 978-0-689-31878-8   ISBN-10: 0-689-31878-2   (hc.)
[1. Death—Fiction. 2. High schools—Fiction. 3. Schools—Fiction. 4. Afro-Americans—Fiction.] I. Title.
PZ7.D78325Te 1994 [Fic]—dc20 94-10278

ISBN-13: 978-0-689-80698-8 (pbk.)
ISBN-10: 0-689-80698-1 (pbk.)

This book is dedicated, with love, to my parents, Victor and Catherine Mills, who gave me wings to fly.

The author gratefully wishes to acknowledge the following people:
Margaret—for her insight, editing, and encouragement
Sandy—for her cheers and her ears
Fred—for his smiles and support
Dr. Kelly—for his psychological expertise
Jeff—for his athletic input
Janell—for her continued belief in me
Jeremy—who is still missed
Vicky—for her gentle spirit
Damon and Cory—my inspirations
Crystal—my Crystal Ballerina
Wendy—my baby girl
All my students who gave me guidance to make it real and finally
Larry—my strength.

A man shrieks in pain
Crying to the universe.
Panic is abrupt.

CRASH, FIRE, PAIN

Newspaper Article

NOVEMBER 8

TEEN BASKETBALL STAR KILLED IN FIERY CRASH

Nov. 8—Robert Washington, age 17, captain of the Hazelwood High School basketball team, was killed last night in a fiery automobile accident on I-75. Witnesses say the car, driven by Andrew Jackson, 17, also of the Hazelwood team, had been noticeably weaving across the lanes of the expressway just before it hit a retaining wall and burst into flames.

Jackson, who police said had been drinking, was taken to Good Samaritan Hospital, where he is being treated for burns and bruises. He is listed in good condition. Two other Hazelwood students, B. J. Carson, 16, and Tyrone Mills, 17, who were also in the car, were treated and released.

The three students who escaped serious injury were able to jump from the four-door Chevy immediately after the accident, say witnesses. Washington, however, who was sitting in the front seat next to the driver, had his feet on the dashboard. The force of the crash sent his feet through the windshield, pinning him inside the automobile. The car's gas tank then exploded. Although Jackson tried frantically to rescue Washington, he and his friends watched helplessly as Robert Washington burned to death.

HIT THE SHOWERS!
HIT THE STREETS!

Locker-Room Conversation
after the Game

—Hey, Rob! Live game, man. You be flyin' with the hoops, man! Swoosh! Ain't nobody better, 'cept maybe me.

—Yo, Andy, my main man! I see you been eatin' bull crap for dinner again! You only *wish* you was as good as me! I, Robert Orlando Washington, will be makin' *billions* of dollars playin' for the N.B.A.! Want me to save you a ticket to one of my games?

—Man, you be trippin'! You better be lookin' out for *me*—here's my card—Andy Jackson—superstar shooter and lover to the ladies—'cause I'm gonna be the high-point man on the opposin' team—the team that wipes the floor with you and your billion dollars!

—Dream on, superstar! Just for that,

3

I'm gonna make you *buy* your ticket!

—Let's get outta here, man, before I feel the need to dust you off. This locker room smell really funky tonight.

—I'm with you, my man Andy. You the one with the raggedy ride. Hey, and when you take them funky basketball shoes and your underarms outta here, I bet this locker room be smellin' like roses.

—You fulla mess, Rob. See, one minute, you makin' plans to keep me outta your N.B.A. games, and the next minute you beggin' a ride in my raggedy wheels. You think the brew is cold, man?

—Yeah, man. It oughta be. We put it in the trunk of your car hours ago—Ain't nothin' like some cool bottled sunshine in the moonlight after a hot game!

—Talk about hot! Didja see my Keisha up in the stands? She had on this short, butt-huggin' skirt, and she kept jumpin' and shakin' every time we scored and . . .

—Well, she did a whole lotta shakin' then! I was in there! No wonder you only scored six tonight. You too busy scopin' the women in the stands. Keisha got your nose wide open. She say "jump" and you say "how high."

—Hey, jumpin' with Keisha is like touchin' the sky. I'd say I had an honorable excuse, my man. Yo, I betcha I score more than six with Keisha tonight!

—That girl got you wrapped and slapped, my man.

—Oooo! Well, slap me some more! Let's raise.

—Hey, Gerald, what's up, man?

—Nothin' much—cold-blooded game, Rob. Twenty-seven points—you be dealin' out there!

—What can I say? College scouts from all over the world are knockin' on my door, beggin' me to drive six new Cadillacs to their school, to instruct the women in the dorms on the finer points of—shall we say—"scorin'"—and to teach skinny little farm boys what it is, what it is!!

—Andy, I don't see why you hang with this big-head fool, except maybe to learn some basketball. What you score tonight—four?

—Hey, Gerald, I thought you was my man. You sound like the coach—and it was six points, thank you. I got more important things on my mind tonight.

—Yeah, maybe Keisha can teach him some basketball! You wanna go with us tonight, Gerald? We got some brew and we just gonna be chillin'.

—Naw, Rob. I got to be gettin' home. And my old man . . . you know how he is. . . . Besides, who would wanna be seen with two dudes named after a couple of dead presidents anyway?

5

—Forget you, man. You seen B. J. and Tyrone?

—Yeah, man. They waitin' for you out by Andy's car. Tyrone went out early to see if he could catch up with Rhonda. He said he wanted to see if she was leavin' with anybody. He ain't called her yet, but he's got that puppy-dog look—kinda like the look on Andy's face when Keisha walks into study hall.

—Naw, man. Ain't no girl got me hooked up. I got her well trained.

—You better not let Keisha hear you say that!

—You got that right!

—Hey, Andy, when you gonna get that raggedy red car of yours painted?

—When my old man gets tired of lookin' at it, I guess. He said something about a reward if my grades get better, but you know how that is.

—Yeah, man. Parents be trippin'. But don't get me talkin' 'bout fathers. He's the reason why I gotta raise outta here now. Where y'all goin'?

—No particular place. We just gonna chill. We might try to find a party, or we might just finish off them beers and let the party find us. Then I'm headin' over to Keisha's house, after I take these turkeys home.

—Don't let Keisha find out you been

drinkin'. I swear, sometimes a girlfriend is worse than a mother!

—Not to worry, Gerald, my man. Besides, we got B. J. with us. He keeps us straight—or at least gives us breath mints.—Ooowee! Them shoes need some breath mints! I'm outta here! Peace.

—Let's raise, Roberto. Tyrone and B. J. gonna freeze to death!

—I'm with you, Andini. Let's heat up the night!

OH NO! IT JUST CAN'T BE!

Phone Calls

NOVEMBER 7
11:00 P.M.

—Hello, may I speak to Keisha, please?

—Keisha, this is Rhonda. Sit down, girl. There's been an accident. Some lady who works at Good Sam with my mother called her a few minutes ago and told her that they had just brought in some kids from Hazelwood— basketball players, she thinks.

—Oh, Rhonda, I just called Andy to find out what was taking him so long. He was supposed to be here an hour ago. There's no answer at his house. I was gonna kill him! You don't think it was Andy, do you?

—I don't know, Keisha. I called Robert's house and all I got was that stupid recording. But then that's all you ever get when you call Rob.

8

—What about Gerald? He usually hangs with them after the game. I'll call him and then I'll call you right back, okay?

—Gerald, this is Keisha. Have you seen Andy?

—Naw, I went home right after the game, but Andy and Rob, and I think Tyrone and B. J. too, left together in Andy's car. Andy said he was comin' by your house after he took those clowns home. He ain't there yet?

—Uh-uh. Well, if he calls you, tell him to get in touch with me right away, okay? Hey, you haven't heard anything about an accident, have you?

—Why is it the first thing a girl thinks about if her boyfriend is late is that he been in an accident? I bet he's in the backseat of his car, kissin' all over some real sexy mama!!

—All you fellas are alike—worthless. Call me if you hear anything, okay?

—Sure. Later.

—Hello, may I speak to Rhonda? Rhonda, is that you? This is Keisha. I hardly recognized your voice. Have you heard anything? . . . Rhonda? What's wrong?

—Oh, Keisha, it's terrible. There was a crash, and the car exploded, and my mother's friend said she thinks at least one of the boys was killed, maybe more. She said the police officer who came in with the ambulance told her that the car involved in the accident was a red Chevette. Isn't that what Andy drives?

—Oh my God. Rhonda, I've got to go. I'll get my mom to drive me to the hospital. Oh, please let them all be okay. I'll call you from the hospital.

—Rhonda, me again. I'm here at the hospital. . . . It's Robbie Washington. He's . . . He's . . . He's dead! Oh, Rhonda, he died in the accident. No, Andy, B. J., and Tyrone are okay. Tyrone and B. J. have already been sent home. Andy has been admitted, but he's not seriously hurt. Rhonda, what are we going to do? I've never known anybody who died before, except my grandmother, and she was old.

—Oh, Keisha, this is so scary. I don't know how to deal with it. Have you talked to Andy?

—No, they wouldn't let me in there. But I saw him through the door. He looked bad— not injured, but his eyes looked funny—I guess he was in shock. I've got to go now. My mom is taking me home. I'll call you tomorrow.

MEMORIES OF FIRE

Tyrone's Statement to Police

NOVEMBER 8

—Tyrone Mills? My name is Officer Casey, and I'd like to ask you a few questions. I understand you were in the car involved in the accident last night. I know you are upset, but it is necessary that we complete this report while the facts are still fresh in your mind. I'd like for you to tell me, in as much detail as possible, what happened last night.

—Well, the game was over 'bout nine-thirty and we was all in a good mood 'cause we won big—by something like forty points, so we was gonna celebrate. Me and B. J. and Andy and . . . and . . . Rob—we left after we all got changed. Gerald was gonna come with us . . . yeah, Gerald Nickelby, but he had to go home. His stepfather beats . . . uh, I mean, his old man is real strict. So it was just the four of us. . . . Naw, B. J. don't play on the team—he's too short, but the four of us hang together. We been tight since seventh grade.

So, we get in the car . . . yeah, Andy's car, and we start drivin' around, you know, just foolin' around, havin' a good time, yellin' out the window at old white ladies—it always freaks 'em out. . . . Yeah, we was drinkin'—all 'cept B. J.—he don't drink. We had put about four six-packs in the trunk of Andy's car before the game. Since the weather's been so cold, puttin' 'em in the trunk was as good as a cooler, so they was nice and frosty by the time we got to 'em. . . . Yeah, all of us was drinkin', 'cept B. J., like I said, but Andy probably had the most. He was in a *real* good mood 'cause this girl named Keisha had started goin' with him and he was goin' over to her house after he took us home.

After a while the car started to sway, but I wasn't sure if it was me gettin' dizzy or if the car really was weaving across the expressway. At the time it seemed really funny. We was laughin' so hard—especially when people started honkin' at us. The more they tried to signal us, and I guess, warn us, the more we was crackin' up and laughin'. Rob had his feet up on the dashboard, partly actin' silly, and partly 'cause his legs was so long that they got cramped in that little car of Andy's. Me and

B. J. was in the backseat. I was sittin' right behind Andy, and B. J. was sittin' next to me, behind Rob, 'cause he had the shortest legs, and Rob could push the seat all the way back.

Then, all of a sudden, like outta nowhere, this wall was in front of us, like it just jumped out in front of the car, and Andy was trying to find the brakes with his foot, and then there was glass everywhere and this crunchin', grindin' sound. My door flew open, and I rolled out. I remember I was cryin' and crawlin' around on my hands and knees—that's the only thing that got hurt on me—I got glass in my hands and in my knees.

I got to my feet, and I helped Andy outta the front seat. His head was bleedin' pretty bad, and he was holdin' his chest like he couldn't breathe so good—I think he hit the steerin' wheel pretty hard. We could smell gas real strong—it made me dizzy—like the gas station smells when some lady don't know when to stop and she spills gas all down the side of her car.

By that time, B. J. had gotten out, and we was lookin' for Rob. He musta passed out at first, 'cause all of a sudden we hear this screamin'. We ran around to that side but the door was bent shut and we couldn't get it open. All of us was screamin' by that time, 'cause we could see his feet stickin' through the windshield. His legs was cut and bleedin' really bad.

All we could see was these brand-new Nikes stickin' out the window, with the rest of Rob screamin' and hollerin', stuck inside.

So then Andy and B. J. climb on top of the car and start to knock pieces of the windshield out of the way, so we can try to get Rob out that way. But then . . . then . . . we hear this heavy, thick sound, like an explosion in a closed room, and Andy and B. J. is knocked off the hood. Me and B. J. grab Andy then, and we have to hold him back, 'cause the whole car is in flames, and Rob is still stuck inside, and we can hear him screamin', "Andy! Andy! Help me—Help me—Oh God, please don't let me die like this! Andy! . . ."

He screamed what seemed like a long time. Then it was real quiet. All we could hear was the sound of the flames, and little pieces of the car sizzlin' and burnin', and then the sirens of the police cars. I think I passed out then. That's what I remember—and that's what I'll never be able to forget.

"DEAR LORD"

B. J.'s Prayer

NOVEMBER 15

—*Dear Lord, this is me, B. J. Carson. You know, the one You made too short. But that's okay; I know You had Your reasons. I know I don't pray very often, and I know You haven't seen me in church lately, but I feel like I need to pray or something. There's some stuff I don't understand about this accident—like why it happened and why Robbie had to die and why I didn't die. Mama keeps huggin' me, sayin', "Praise the Lord" and stuff like that. But what about Robbie's mama? What is she saying?*

Is it my fault that Robbie is dead? I wasn't drivin'. I wasn't even drinkin'. Andy and Rob and Tyrone all knew that I didn't drink—they never bothered me much about it. I think they even respected me a little because of it. I told them that drinking at an early age had stunted my growth, so I had given it up in favor of other vices. (Actually I think beer tastes like boiled sweat socks.) So they knew not to push me. Maybe that's all I have left over from those days when I used to go to church every Sunday with Mama. So why do I feel so guilty?

I don't sleep so good at night. I keep seein' the fire and hearin' his screams and feelin' so helpless. He was too young to die like that. It's not fair. He never had a chance. Was all this done to teach us kids a lesson? Will it stop us from drinkin' and drivin'? Maybe—a few. But the rest will keep on doing it, no matter what. So I still don't understand why.

Mama says the Lord knows all, and that He in His infinite wisdom knows the reason for all things. But Mama is gettin' old, and she's known a lot of people who've died, so she probably understands all this death stuff a whole lot better than I do.

Maybe I shoulda tried to stop them that night. Maybe I shoulda been drivin'. But I'm always so glad that they include me in their group, I hardly ever try to change their plans. I'm just glad to go along. Actually, I never really understood why they like me. They're all tall, popular with the girls, and basically outrageous. Me, I'm short—never once made the basketball team—kinda quiet, and still unsure of myself when it comes to girls. But somehow, I was always "one of the boys"—and the four of us did everything together, ever since seventh grade. And I've just been glad that I had such good friends. Now one of them is gone and I feel responsible.

I think I'll go to church with Mama this Sunday. I know people will say that it's because of the accident that I came back to church— well, they're right. I'm not too proud to know when a problem is bigger than I am. Of course most things in life are bigger than I am, but I'm learnin' to live with it.

Please, Lord, help me to learn to live with this too. Thanks for listenin'. See you Sunday.

"MY MOST FRIGHTENING MOMENT"

Rhonda's English Homework

NOVEMBER 16

Rhonda Jeffries
English Homework
November 16
Personal Essay
Topic—My Most Frightening Moment

    Last week I learned that kids my age could die. That was the most frightening experience I ever had. A boy that I knew real well, that sat next to me in study hall, died in a car crash.

    It all started at school on the day before the basketball game. We were all sitting around on the steps of the school, talking about nothing, really. I think Gerald was complaining how ugly everything looked—there were no leaves on the trees, and everything was all muddy from the last time it had snowed. Our school building must have been built about a million years ago, because it was brown and tall and raggedy-looking, but it fit right in with the rest of the day.

Then Robbie said he knew how to brighten up any day. He talked about "bottles of sunshine" that were sitting there on the shelves of the liquor store on 4th Street. Andy said he knew how to get some beer and he'd have it the next day after the game. The bell rang then and we went to class. I forgot all about the conversation until I heard on the news that Robbie had been killed.

The next day everybody at school was crying—even the people who didn't know Robbie, even the teachers. That's all everybody talked about all day long. They even had TV cameras here, getting close-ups of kids crying and stuff.

I didn't cry. I felt really sick inside—and mad at Andy and them for drinking in the first place. I thought we'd all come back for our reunions and then we'd get old, and then, when we're so old it doesn't matter anymore, we'd die. But he's dead already. I didn't think it was possible. And that's why it's so scary.

THE HAZELWOOD HERALD

NOVEMBER 16 *** SPECIAL EDITION

IN MEMORIUM

Robbie Washington, captain of our basketball team, was killed after the November 7 game in a terrible automobile accident.

A memorial service was held here at school last week where students, teammates, and staff expressed their grief.

Robbie always had a cheerful grin and a positive attitude. He was a talented athlete, and an honor student as well. Hazelwood will miss you, Robbie.

Canned Food Drive Begins

The annual canned food drive, which is sponsored by the Unity Cultural Association, will continue through the Christmas holidays. The period from the Thanksgiving holidays through the Christmas season is traditionally a time when we become aware of those who are less fortunate. Each student is asked to bring at least 5 canned goods. The class that brings in the most will be given a pizza party sponsored by the U.C.A. This is a time when all cultural groups of our school work together for the betterment of man.

International Guests

Last week, a group of students from French West Africa visited Hazelwood as part of the International Exchange Experience. They visited Madame Loisel's advanced French classes and amazed the students with their vast knowledge of not only French, but also English, Swahili, and several African dialects.

When asked what she thought about our school, Niafra Abundada, 16, replied, "Because your school is very large, very old, and very crowded, it frightened me at first. But even though I feel that the American students do not give enough honor to their teachers, I envy your freedom of expression, and I appreciate the friendship that you have shown me."

The exchange students will return to their country after a visit to New York City.

BUS CHANGES

Students who ride the yellow buses are reminded that fighting and other undignified behavior will result in a suspension from the bus and a possible suspension from school. Vice Principal Leo Davis has said that all incidents of disorderly conduct and unruly behavior must be eliminated in order to insure the safety of all concerned.

Editorial Comments

Last week, there were 400 people in the Senior Class. Today there are 399. One student became a statistic when he lost his life in an accident involving drinking and driving. Usually, statistics don't mean much, but this statistic had a name, a face, a basketball jersey, and friends. Every 18 minutes, every day of the year, someone is killed in a drunk-driving accident. Alcohol-related fatalities are the number one cause of death in teenagers. When will we learn?

On Giving Thanks

As we approach the Thanksgiving season and start to collect canned goods for the poor (as if they are not hungry for the other eleven months of the year), we should all look around, and instead of complaining like we usually do, sit down, and truly give thanks for the blessings that we have been given. We are accustomed to whining about how small our allowances are, or how upset we are because we only have three pairs of athletic shoes, when there are so many around us who have *no* money, no homes, and no shoes at all. In addition, we have family and friends that care about us and we have the hope of a bright future. And, because we have learned that death is close by and can touch us, we must give thanks for the simplest and greatest blessing of all—life.

SPORTS SCENE

Loss Stuns Tigers

The Hazelwood basketball team returned for its first practice yesterday since the death of captain Robbie Washington. Team members filed quietly into the locker room where Coach Ripley talked to them for over an hour. The team decided to forfeit the next two games and to dedicate the rest of the season to Rob and to try to win the title as a tribute to him. Andy Jackson was chosen as new team captain.

Ski Trip All Downhill

Let's face it. Most of us are city kids and we just don't ski much. Last week 51 students on an Ecology Club trip experienced the thrills of downhill skiing. Jean Gill, gr. 11, said, "I'll be back. It was live!"

TEACHER OF THE WEEK
Coach Mark Ripley

This week we feature Mr. Ripley, head coach of the Hazelwood track and basketball teams. He began coaching 10 years ago and has led our basketball team to the city finals 6 times and to the state finals twice. He is married and has one son. Coach Ripley is very popular with the athletes, as well as the other students. He always has time to stop and listen if someone has a problem. He sponsors two S.A.D.D. groups—Students Against Driving Drunk and Student Athletes Detest Drugs.

"HEY, COACH! CAN WE TALK?"

Andy's First Day Back to School

NOVEMBER 19

—Hey, Coach, what's doin'?

—How are you, Andy? How was your first day back to school?

—Not so good, Coach. It was rough. I feel okay, I mean, I ain't really busted up that bad. I got a few bruises and burns left over on the outside of me, but the inside of me is hurtin'. You know what I mean?

—I hear you, man. It's a rough scene to handle. How about your friends and your family? They're behind you, aren't they?

—Yeah, I guess. Me and B. J. and Tyrone'll never be the same, but we'll always be real tight because of this. And the other kids are tryin' real hard to be understandin'. My folks—well, you know how it is. My dad keeps

23

tellin' me to be strong and put this all behind me. My mom won't really look at me. She cries a lot, but she hasn't said much about the accident after that first night.

—What about *you*, Andy? How do *you* feel about all this? This is quite a bit for you to handle.

—I'm okay.

—C'mon now. You just said you felt like you were hurting inside. What's going on?

—Well, if you really want to know, I wanted to die right after the accident. I wanted it to be me that was dead instead of Rob. He had so much goin' for himself. He woulda got that scholarship too, Coach. You know he woulda. He woulda made it big in the pro's too. He was 6 feet 5 inches and still growing. And he was my friend.

—You can't blame yourself forever, Andy. And if you had died instead of Rob, would you want *him* to be hurting like you are now?

—I don't know. I'm all mixed up.

—How long have you and Rob been friends?

—I remember the first time I saw him— tallest kid in the seventh grade. He and Tyrone were best friends from elementary school and they went around callin' each other "Tyronio" and "Roberto" like some kind of weirdos or something. Later on they started callin' me "Andini," but it was never as cool as their names because Andrew just didn't sound good endin' with an "o." You know what I mean?

—Yeah, I hear you.

—After I got to know them, and the three of us started hangin' together, I decided it didn't sound so bad. Anyway, the first day I saw him, he was pickin' his hair out with his red pick with diamond-lookin' things on it. I went over to him, and said, "Won't yo' mama get mad when she finds out you took her pick?" He slowly put the pick in his back pocket, slowly looked at me, and then proceeded to beat the snot out of me. We've been tight ever since.

—Nothing like a good fight to start out a solid friendship.

—Me and Rob and Tyrone had most of our classes together, and even went out for the junior high basketball team together. B. J. tried out too, but he didn't make it. I guess you know, Coach, that B. J. has tried out for basketball every year for six years, including junior high, and never made it once. He keeps sayin' he's gonna be the next Spud Webb.

—Yeah, that B. J. is something else.

—He's got more guts than I'll ever have. It was B. J.'s idea to try to climb on the hood to rescue Rob. Like I said, he's the one with the guts.

—From what I hear, you have your share of guts and courage too. Without you, the other boys may have been injured much more than they were. Wasn't it you that helped get Tyrone and B. J. out of the car?

—Don't believe everything you hear. I think it was the other way around. Actually, I don't really remember. . . . but I couldn't get to Robbie. I couldn't get to Robbie.

—That's right. You *couldn't.* There are some things that are beyond our power to control.

—I coulda controlled the drinkin'. I knew better. We all did. We just never figured it would happen to us.

—I hear you.

—I never will know why I didn't get hurt worse—I shoulda been hurt so bad that at least I had to stay for a couple of months—but they let me go home in two days. My burns weren't too bad.

—Well, except for the miscellaneous Band-Aids, I'd say you look pretty good, considering. Have you recuperated from that court ordeal yet?

—After I got out of the hospital, and after all the police investigations, and I found out that I had to go to court, I was really scared. I really appreciate you comin' down there, Coach.

—No problem, kid. Just wanted to let you know we're all behind you.

—I was surprised so many kids from school was there—all the kids from S.A.D.D., several other teachers. Of course, Rob's parents, my parents, and Keisha was there. It was almost as bad as the funeral. When the judge talked to me, and I cried, in front of everybody, I was kinda embarrassed, but I guess that was okay—I guess they understood. A lot of them was cryin' too.

—I was too, Andy. There's no shame in tears.

—Coach, can you explain somethin' to me?

—Sure, Andy, if I can.

—I had been charged with DWI and vehicular homicide, but they dropped the vehicular homicide charge because of my age and good-driving record. I ended up gettin' my license revoked until I'm twenty-one, and a two-year suspended sentence. Even I thought it was a real easy sentence, maybe too easy. Do you think that was right? Shouldn't I been sent to jail or somethin'?

—The judge did what he thought was best in your case, Andy. You gotta stop punishing yourself.

—I think I would have felt better if I woulda had to suffer and complain a little.

—You *are* suffering, Andy. The judge knows that. We all do. And we'll help you all we can. You come see me whenever you need to talk, okay?

—Yeah, man. Thanks. When can I play ball again?

—What does your doctor say?

—I have nothin' broken—just some slight burns, a few cuts, and a couple of ugly bruises. When I was in the hospital, they ran all these tests, but everything came out okay. They told me I was lucky. . . . Yeah, right.

—Don't you have to go to the Health Clinic for your Alcohol Rehabilitation classes?

—Yeah, I go every Saturday from six in the morning till six at night.

—Wow, that's a long day.

—Yeah. They said they wanted my attention *first* thing in the morning. Well, they sure got it. That's even earlier than I leave for school. I went to the first one last week. It wasn't so bad. Actually, I learned a lot.

—Did you talk to the counselors there about returning to normal school activities, including basketball? Games start at eight, you know. Can you make it on Saturday?

—Yeah, no problem. They said they wanted me to have as normal a school life as possible. It's not like those programs that take away all your privileges completely. So I asked them about sports, and they said that as long as I didn't miss any sessions over there and was able to keep my grades somewhere above basement level, I could play basketball again. I'd like to try, Coach.

—It's been tough on all of us, Andy. We haven't had a practice, and we've forfeited two games since the . . . accident. But I feel that it's time to move on. I think Robbie would have wanted us to keep playing, don't you?

—Yeah, I think he woulda.

—We'll have our first practice tomorrow. I'll see you then.

—Thanks, Coach . . . for everythin'.

SAD SONGS, JUICY GOSSIP

Rhonda's Letter to Her Friend

NOVEMBER 22

November 22

Dear Saundra,

Well, how is California treating you? Do you like it any better since you moved? My dad won't let me call you long distance anymore since we talked all night last month. The bill came to over $200.00 and he was ready to kill me. Even after that great Thanksgiving meal we had yesterday, he wouldn't give in. He just doesn't understand that when your best friend moves 2,000 miles away, you just have to do a lot of catching up. I've got so much to tell you——just wait until you hear what happened at school.

Two weeks ago, right after a basketball game, Robbie Washington got killed in a car accident. It was awful. Andy Jackson was driving, and B. J. Carson and Tyrone Mills were also in the car. Those three got out okay, but Robbie, he got burned to death 'cause the car blew up or something. Every-

body at school was crying and they had this special memorial service for Rob. Then these people from downtown called "grief counselors" came to talk to us. We were supposed to "share" our sorrow with them. Yeah, right. Mostly they sat around and looked concerned and smiled a lot. What seemed to help us the most was us talking in small groups with our friends and some of the teachers. It's going to be rough getting over this. Hardly any of us ever knew anybody who had died before. You kinda figure if you're 17, you'll live forever. But Robbie didn't. That's scary.

Anyway, I told you that I've been kinda liking Tyrone ever since school started, but he never paid me much attention. Well, he called me the day after the accident and we talked for about three hours. (Good thing it wasn't long distance!) He told me how the police questioned him, and how bad he felt, and how he was glad to have me (me!!) to talk to. He told me he thought I was cute, but he didn't want to bother me because he thought I was going with Gerald. (Be for _real!_) I told him that me and Gerald were just friends. Gerald's cousin, Latrice (Remember her? The one who got pregnant?), and my older sister, Jackie, were best friends, so me and Gerald knew each other pretty well. But I never even considered going with him. So I told Tyrone all this, and he asked me if he could come over on that Saturday. So, we've been talking pretty regular ever since then. I still can't get over it——he is so fine!

Andy and Keisha are still hooked up. She said to tell you hi next time I write to you. She said Andy is having a hard time adjusting to the accident. I guess I would too, if I was driving and my best friend had gotten killed. He gets these crying spells, she said, and gets real depressed. His mother is sending him to a shrink, I heard. As far as I'm concerned, his mama needs a shrink. When she comes to the basketball games, which isn't often, she wears high heels and a silk dress and a full-length leather coat; all the other mothers wear sweat suits and jogging shoes. She always seems uncomfortable there——like the noise of the game offends her or something. I don't remember his dad ever showing up at all.

Well, I'm getting one of those sore spots on my finger from writing all this. If anything else happens this exciting, I'm going to just have to sneak and call you anyway. My dad won't really kill me——he just hollers a lot. I'm sending you the last issue of <u>The Hazelwood Herald</u> so you can catch up on the rest of the school stuff. Write back as soon as you can. I hope you had a great Thanksgiving.

Love,
Rhonda

P.S. Girl, that Tyrone can really kiss!!!!!!!!! Makes me want to stand up and shout Hallelujah!

"IF I COULD CHANGE THE WORLD"

Gerald's English Homework

NOVEMBER 29

Gerald Nickelby
English Homework
November 29

Personal Essay
Topic—If I Could Change the World

    If I could change the world I'd get rid of peanut butter, Band-Aids, and five-dollar bills. I know this sounds like a weird list, but I got my reasons.

    First, I'd get rid of peanut butter. When I was little, peanut butter and jelly was my favorite kind of sandwich. Mama would fix it as a special treat and it always made my lunch box smell so good. But Mama left and the peanut butter stayed. We get it free, so there's jars of it sitting around. Sometimes that's all there is. It sticks to my teeth and it seems like it sticks my bones together—it always makes me feel clogged up.

I'd also get rid of Band-Aids—for two reasons. One, they're beige. They say on the box, "skin tone" is the color of the bandages inside. Whose skin? Not mine! So I HATE wearing Band-Aids because they're so noticeable and people always say, "How'd you get that cut, or that bruise, or those stitches?" And I always have to make up a reason about how I hurt myself. When Andy came back to school after the accident, he was wearing a bunch of Band-Aids. At least it took the attention away from me for a while. But I'd still eliminate Band-Aids—at least beige ones.

Finally, I'd get rid of five-dollar bills. With a five-dollar bill, somebody's stepfather can buy a bottle of whiskey, a nickel bag of pot, or a rock of crack. He smokes it, or drinks it, and goes home and knocks his kids around, or his wife (before she got sick of it and left). He makes his kids wish they could leave. The next morning he doesn't even remember what he did. With a five-dollar bill, Andy and the guys bought a six-pack of beer. They ended up buying five dollars worth of death. It seems like all a five spot can do is buy trouble, so I'd get rid of five-dollar bills.

So, to make MY world better, I'd get rid of peanut butter, Band-Aids, and five-dollar bills.

HOOPS AND DUNKS

The Big Basketball Game

DECEMBER 7

—Okay, okay. Everybody here? Where's Jackson? Anybody seen Jackson?

—I called his house, Coach, to give him a ride, but his little brother said he already left. He said Andy was takin' the bus.

—The bus? Good grief, he may never get here! All right, let's go over the game plan. This is a big one for us, and I know it's our first home game since . . . since we lost Robbie, so it's going to be difficult for all of us—especially Andy. Let's see if we can give him as much support out there as we can—assuming he gets here. The bus! I could have picked him up if he had called me.

—He's been real moody lately, Coach.

Sometimes he just likes to be alone. He don't talk to us like he used to.

—I know. I've been trying—

—Hey, Coach! Andy's here!

—Great. I was getting worried, Andy. Are you ready to play?

—Sure. No problem. Let's get it on!

—Okay, get suited up and meet me on the court for warm-ups in three minutes. We have a game to win!

—. . . and we now have only four minutes, thirty-three seconds remaining in the second half and Hazelwood trails by eight. This has been a very emotional game for all involved. The Tigers really want to win this one because this is their first home game since that devastating loss of their popular and capable center, Robbie Washington.

And it's a pass to Jackson, to Mills, back to Jackson and it's in for two.

That's fourteen points now for Jackson, Hazelwood's new center. It's hard to fill another man's shoes, but he's wearing them tonight.

Covedale's Stefanski is ready to move the ball downcourt—he tries one from the outside—it's good. The score is now 62-54. Hazelwood's Mills takes it down, under full-court pressure, and—no—he's fouled on the shot and will go to the line for two.

Mills has ten points in this game so far—

make that eleven—Now let's see how he does on this next one—He takes his time, pulls the trigger—and he's got it! That gives him twelve, and brings Hazelwood within six. Covedale takes the ball out. Jackson steals and drives for the basket. It rolls on the rim—and it is—good! He's dynamite tonight!

The score now stands at 62-58 and we've got about three minutes remaining in the game. Covedale takes it down. Barkley tries an eight-footer and it's no good. Hazelwood seems to be on fire and Covedale out of steam as Shuttlesworth drives it hard on the inside, fakes the jump shot, and finger rolls it in for an easy two points.

Hazelwood is now within two points of tying the score with Covedale, but no, Covedale's big man, Stefanski, who never seems to miss, gets two and the score is 64-60, with 1:04 remaining.

The ball is passed now to Mills, to Shuttlesworth, and to Jackson who seems almost frenzied out there. He grabs the ball, gets up close, and *dunks* it in! The crowd is going wild! You can hear the thunder of the stomping feet in the stands as they cheer and stomp, giving their team their noisy, enthusiastic support.

There're fourteen seconds left to play and Hazelwood is still down by two. Covedale's Macintosh drives it down, tries for three, and—it rolls off the rim. The crowd is roaring!

Billy Smith grabs it for Hazelwood and passes it to Mills. Mills can't find an opening. The clock is running—the crowd is counting—ten seconds, nine, eight . . . He throws it off to Jackson, who is blocked by Stefanski. Jackson turns—he's got one clear shot, but *he has never made a three-pointer in his high school career!* There's six seconds, five—he shoots—it touches the rim—it rolls around—two seconds—*it's in!* . . . and it's good!

The crowd is spilling out of the stands and onto the floor. They're screaming and cheering and mobbing the team, who pulled out a fantastic win tonight. Andy Jackson should be very proud of himself. He proved that he could stand up under pressure and in spite of the severe emotional strain he must have been under, he was able to pull it out. Congratulations to Jackson and to the Hazelwood team for a stunning 65-64 victory over Covedale. This is station WTLZ bringing you the high school game of the week.

—Good night, Coach! See ya Monday.

—Good night, Tyrone. Great game, son. Are you the last one out? I'm ready to lock up and get out of here.

—No, Andy's still gettin' changed. I guess he's takin' his time, tryin' to make this night last a little longer. I offered him a ride, but he said he was waitin' for his dad.

—Okay, thanks Tyrone. Tell Rhonda I said hello.

—How'd you know?

—Didn't you know I was a psychic with X-ray vision?

—Hey, I thought that was just my mom. Later, Coach.

—Later, man. See you at practice Monday. . . . Andy—you still here?

—Over here, Coach. I just have to get my shoes. I was waitin' for my dad—he said he'd be here.

—You played a terrific game tonight, Andy. I'm sure your dad was popping with pride.

—He wasn't poppin' with nothin'. He didn't come. He never comes. He always says he will, but there's always an excuse.

—What about your mom? Was she there?

—No, she doesn't like basketball—too noisy—too sweaty—somethin' like that. You know what? Rob's parents were at the game. It must have been awfully hard for them. But they *always* came to our games, even the away games. It's like they supported not just Rob, but the whole team. Seein' them up there really made us want to win tonight—it made us not want to give up. They sat there, Rob's mom holdin' back tears, and my folks didn't even bother to show up. *I* should be the one dead, not Rob.

—That's not true, and you know it, Andy.

It's hard for us to understand why things like this happen, and I think you're doing a remarkable job of handling a very rough situation. You came back to the team, you're playing well—and we all support you. You know that. Actually, *you* are the glue that's holding the team together. Without you, we'd all fall apart.

—I don't see how. I'm not even holdin' myself together very well. I just don't understand so much stuff. I just can't—

—Go ahead and cry, Andy. Don't be afraid of those tears. Sometimes they help to wash the soul clean. . . . Come on, I'll take you home.

"HOW DO I FEEL?"

Andy's First Visit to the Psychologist

DECEMBER 10

—Andy, my name is Dr. Carrothers. I'm glad you were able to come today. Are you comfortable?

—Yeah, I guess. Hey, man. I ain't never seen no black shrink before.

—Well, here I am. I went to the University of Cincinnati for my undergraduate and master's degrees. And I got my Ph.D. from Yale.

—Man, I can't even pass chemistry. You make a buncha cash?

—Over ninety dollars an hour.

—That's heavy, man. I'm impressed. You must be real smart. I can't even spell "psychiatrist."

—I'm no smarter than you are, Andy. I struggled through high school. I worried about my math grades, and I always had trouble in

English composition classes. But I kept going, and I found out that it wasn't impossible. In college, it got easier, once I figured out that I was as capable as the next dude—maybe more so. And I'm a psychologist, not a psychiatrist.

—What's the difference?

—They make more money. No, just kidding. They can dispense medication, and I don't. There's a couple of other differences, but that's basically it.

—And you think you can help me?

—Let's say that I'm going to try to help you help yourself. I'm no magician.

—That's fair. But I still don't think I need to be here, 'specially at almost a hundred dollars an hour. Who's payin' for this, anyway?

—Your dad's insurance, mostly. They feel it's worth it.

—Yeah, I guess they would.

—Now, we both know that your parents have requested this counseling for you, even though you say it's not necessary. They're very concerned that the automobile accident in which you were involved may have affected you more than you are aware. We know why *they* want you to be here. Why do *you* think you're here?

—'Cause I'm depressed. But I don't need a shrink, not even a smart black shrink. I'm fine. School is fine. Everythin's just cool. Can I go now?

—I'll tell you what, Andy. If, at the end of this hour, you have convinced me that everything is really fine, you don't have to come back, bet?

—Bet.

—Okay, take your time, and just tell me what has happened in your life since that night. It doesn't have to make sense—just let the thoughts come as they come. Talk to me, Andy. What we say here doesn't go out of these doors. That's a promise. You'll be surprised how much better you will feel if you just talk about some of the jumbled up thoughts in your head.

—Well, if you say so. But I really am okay now. I have headaches sometimes, and I can't sleep some nights, but I feel a whole lot better than I did right after the accident.

—How did you feel then?

—Like a piece of crap.

—Why?

—'Cause it was my fault that Rob died.

—Why do you say that?

—I was drinkin'. I was drivin'.

—Do you think Rob blames you?

—I don't know. Probably not. He was such a cool dude. He took everythin' real easy. Nothin' hardly ever upset him.

—So maybe you're blaming yourself for something that Rob forgives you for.

—Maybe.

—What was it like when you first went back to school?

—Most of my friends were very understandin', and most of my teachers were cool—as cool as teachers can get—they *do* have their limits, you know. Some of 'em smiled a lot. Most of 'em just kept pilin' on the homework like nothin' had happened. None of 'em ever took the time to sit down and talk to me, and ask me if I was havin' any problems, except Coach Ripley. He's an okay dude.

—He's your basketball coach?

—Yeah. But like I said, I don't really care. I can take it.

—You can take what? Did you get any negative reactions from people at school?

—There were a few bad things that happened—like the note I found taped to my locker that said, "Killer!" And the kids who wouldn't look at me in the face. I never figured out if they was embarrassed or angry, but most people adjusted.

—How did you feel about that? The note on your locker. Do you think you're a killer?

—Naw, man. I ain't no killer. I never wanted to hurt nobody. But he's just as dead. What difference does it make?

—It makes a lot of difference, Andy. Don't you think Robbie knows that you didn't mean to hurt him?

44

—I don't know, man. And I sure can't ask Robbie, can I?

—Why not? Pretend I'm Rob. Ask me.

—You ain't Rob.

—I know that and you know that and even Rob knows that. But let's just try it and see what happens. Ask Rob if he blames you.

—I'm sorry, Rob. How can I ever make you know how sorry I am?

—I know you are, Andy. It's okay. Really. I don't blame you. Maybe all of this was meant to be. We can't always see the big picture, you know.

—Yeah, man. But it's rough. . . . Hey, that's enough of this stupid pretendin'.

—Okay. That was great. Tell me about basketball. What's that been like for you without Rob?

—How do you know about me and basketball? You workin' from a script?

—No, Andy. In my initial interview with your parents, they shared with me what they thought was important to your life—things like basketball. It was all very surface information. There's a lot about you that they don't really know.

—You ain't lyin' there, man. You could talk to them all day and never find out anythin' about me.

—Do you think your parents understand your problems?

—Heckee, no! Sometimes I think my parents ain't got no grip on reality. My mother lives in "la-la land." Do you know that she still says "Negro" and refuses to call us black or African-American? At least she doesn't say "colored." She says that her skin is *not* black and never will be and that she doesn't know anyone from Africa; why should she change what has worked perfectly well all of her life? I've given up tryin' to convert her.

—What kinds of things is she interested in?

—She's active in her sorority activities, which to me seems kinda stupid. You got a bunch of black women (forgive me, Mother), who graduated from college twenty-five years ago, who meet once a month to talk about the good old days. That reminds me—she keeps the station on her car radio set to one of those oldies stations. If I hear the Supremes one more time, I think I'll scream!

—Does she ever listen to *your* music?

—Be for real! Anyway, they plan meaningless activities like cotillions for girls like Rhonda and Keisha. She once asked me if I would like to be an escort for one of the girls.

—What'd you say?

—I almost died! Me? Put on a tuxedo and dance the waltz with some pimply faced girl whose major goal in life is to master the bass trombone? I don't think so. So me and my mom kinda stay out of each other's way. We don't dislike each other—we just don't think alike.

—What about your dad?

—My dad is another one who can't deal with the real world, although he doesn't think so. He's active in the Republican party—yes, I said "Republican." Isn't that disgustin'?

—If you say so.

—He's got a good job workin' at Proctor and Gamble, where his main function, as far as I can tell, is kissin' up to white people. He's the vice president of somethin' or other—some office they created when affirmative action was real popular. He's got a car phone and a fax machine—I guess he thinks he's got it made. But he doesn't make it to very many of my basketball games—too busy, or out of town, usually.

—Does that bother you?

—Yeah, sometimes.

—Do you think he realizes how that hurts you?

—Man, he hasn't got the slightest idea what I think about or care about. He once told me that he hoped I'd go into the business world with him when I finished college. But I plan to use my lips for kissin' beautiful women, not the soles of some bald-headed white man's feet. You know, I can't even remember the last time he was in my room. He yells at me through the door every once in a while to turn my music down, but he never comes in. I wonder why.

—Why don't you ask him?

—Naw, man. I ask him a question, and I get a lecture. I gave up askin' him questions when I was twelve years old. It's easier that way.

—What about your little brother?

—Now you talkin'. The only one in my family who is really cool is my little brother, Monty. But I worry about him. I think when he gets to be my age, he's goin' to have a lot of problems. I know he's only six, but he doesn't think black is cool. And he's got this thing for little girls with yellow hair—yeah, I worry about the kid sometimes.

—Are your parents concerned?

—My parents are no help—they don't even know there *is* a problem, let alone how to solve it. Monty gets a lot of attention from them, though, more than they ever gave me. I'm not jealous, but I think they like him better. He's still cute and charmin' and hasn't started to get rebellious or misunderstood yet.

—Like you?

—Like me.

—So, how's it going, now that you're playing ball again?

—It was hard at first gettin' used to Rob's empty seat at school and goin' by his locker. But basketball, instead of bein' harder, got easier. It's like I could work out my feelings on the basketball court. The coach gave me his position—center.

—How'd you feel about that?

—I felt proud, but I also felt a little guilty because I never coulda *won* that position from him. He was the best center that Hazelwood ever had.

—So why did you accept the position?

—I decided that he woulda wanted me to have it, so I worked really hard, and I really improved my game. I'm averaging seventeen points a game.

—That's good. Do you feel good or guilty when you have a good game?

—Probably a little of both.

—I'd say that's normal. Tell you what, Andy. Come back next week, and let's talk about school. Bet?

—If you say so. I thought I didn't have to come back. There's not much to say about school, anyway.

—Well, I'd like to talk to you a bit more, if it's okay with you. I really have enjoyed meeting you and talking with you. I'm looking forward to our next conversation.

—Later, man.

GIRL PROBLEMS?

Andy and Keisha
after School

DECEMBER 13

—Hi, Andy. You ready to go? If we don't hurry, we'll miss the bus.

—What I miss is my car.

—Look, you don't have practice, and you don't have a class or a session to go to today. It's kinda nice, to just spend some time together.

—Hey, you look good, Keisha. How come you don't wear a dress more often?

—If I had known you'd notice, I'd wear them every day.

—Oh, I notice, sweet thing. I notice.

—You sure are in a good mood. What's up?

—I don't know. Somehow I feel like I can breathe today. Let's walk home.

—You crazy! You know it's twenty degrees out there? And snowing!

—Okay, okay. The woman has no sense of adventure. How 'bout if we ride the bus out to the mall and catch a movie? We can go to the early show and still get home in time for dinner.

—I wish I could, Andy, but I got a chemistry test tomorrow, plus I got to finish that composition for English class. It's gonna take me all night and then some to get everything done. Then I told my mother that I'd start dinner for her tonight 'cause she has to work late. I just can't tonight, Andy. Can we go this weekend?

—Be like that, then! See if I care! All I ask for is a little of your time, and you want to get all righteous on me. I'll go to the movies by myself!

—Andy, you have that chemistry test tomorrow too. Call me later and we can go over some of the key stuff. Okay? I gotta go. I don't have time to deal with your temper tantrums.

—Hey, I'm sorry, Keisha. I was just lookin' forward to spendin' some time with you. It was *your* idea.

—But I was talking about right now. You want the whole night. I'm not mad, Andy. But you're starting to get on my nerves. Don't forget your chemistry book. I'll talk to you later.

SCHOOL BLUES

Overheard in the Hall between Classes

DECEMBER 14

—Hey, Gerald, whatcha got next bell?

—American history. Killer Killian's givin' a test. And I don't know *nothin'* 'bout no Civil War, Andy.

—She givin' a test? Today?

—Yeah, Andy. I just remembered. You got your book?

—Naw, man. You outta luck. It's too late to study now anyway.

—I don't care. If I can get a D, that'll do. Hey, Tyrone, you catch Arsenio on TV last night?

—Sure did, Gerald, my man. It was just comin' on when I got in from my job at Burger King. The ladies in that singin' group he had on are so fine!

—For real!

—Didja read that story for English homework, Ty?

—Naw, man. Even if she gives a quiz, I'm cool. I sit next to Tiffany Brown, the smartest girl in the world.

—I hear you. I hope she has a class discussion. Then I can catch up on my sleep.

—No chance, today, Andy. I heard she's givin' out midterm notices in class today. I know she got one specially engraved for me.

—Oh no! So close to Christmas! Santa can just skate on by my house! I had my mama just about ready to buy me that leather coat.

—Kiss it good-bye, Andini! Now, if you did your homework every once in a while, like my man Marcus over there, you could wear leather down to your underwear!

—Yeah, man. What can I say? I can't be doin' all that. There's the bell. Let's raise up.

—Peace.

FEROCIOUS FRUSTRATION

Andy's Second Visit
with the Psychologist

DECEMBER 17

—Hello again, Andy. How've you been?

—Not bad. Just hangin' in there.

—Making it to school every day?

—Yeah, I get there. I don't do much while I'm there. All I look forward to is basketball practice.

—Your grades slipping?

—You know those giant slides they have at the swimmin' pool? That's my grades. But then my grades were never that great to start with. My parents are always yellin' at me to improve my grades 'cause I'll never get into college, but then my parents yell at me all the time.

—Do you feel much pressure from your parents?

—Yeah, lately. Since I been gettin' closer to college, they always be on my back.

—Does that bother you?

—Yeah, it does. Sometimes I really do try hard, but it seems like my brain freezes over or somethin'. I just can't learn some of that stuff. And my parents just don't understand that. They want me to be this straight-A superstar and I just can't do that.

—Do you feel that their expectations are too high?

—I don't know. My friend Gerald—his dad beats him—he's got this big scar on his face from when he had to get stitches when his dad knocked him against a radiator. My parents don't beat me, but they don't understand me either.

—What is it they don't understand?

—It's hard to put into words. There's this kid in my class named Marcus who *always* makes good grades. We call him the "curve buster." All the other brothers in class be makin' Cs and Ds. My man Marcus be pullin' As on a regular basis. Instead of that makin' him popular, we all hate him.

—Why do you think that's true?

—'Cause he's doin' somethin' that all our parents have told us we could do, but somehow we just *can't*. It's like easier to just "make do," to get by. I like gettin' good grades, but my friends talk about me if I get called up to the front on Awards Day with all the white kids. It's easier to sit in the back of the auditorium, and laugh, and make hootin' noises when people like Mary Alice Applesapple go up to get their Honor Roll awards.

—What do you think your dad would think of kids like Marcus or Mary Alice?

—He'd probably want me to *marry* the girl. And I'd get a big speech about Marcus and how black youngsters need to achieve and how we got to work so hard to show ourselves better than the white students. I've heard it a million times.

—But your dad's speeches don't have any meaning for you?

—Look, when my dad was seventeen, he was already out of school and workin' fulltime in the mail room of Proctor and Gamble. He didn't have to worry 'bout gettin' into college, because the chance wasn't there. And he didn't have to worry about scholarships or stupid school counselors or just plain feelin' useless.

—I bet he had his share of feeling useless. Have you ever talked to him about it?

—Naw, man. My dad don't *talk*. He lectures, he preaches, he yells. But we don't ever just *talk*.

—What about your counselors at school? Are they any help? If I remember, when I was in high school, the counselor was there to help kids out who had academic problems, or problems at home.

—You had counselors who would talk to black students and see their point of view and help them out?

—No, you're right. It was probably even worse when I was in school. I just happened to be fortunate enough to find a lady who recognized a spark in me and gave me some direction.

—I don't know what it was like back then, but all my counselor be doin' is makin' up schedules and callin' people out of class, as far as I can tell. We got one or two that maybe I could talk to, but they're assigned to another grade level. I'm stuck with the one I got.

—Have you ever talked to your counselor?

—Yeah, once, I did. It was a waste of time. I went to see her about graduation requirements and that kind of stuff. She's this wrinkled old bat with bad breath, so kids avoid her. I tried to sit downwind of her breath, but it was right after lunch and she kept burpin' little bursts of garlic. It was really gross. So I was tryin' to get out of there as quick as possible, and she's givin' me this speech about career goals, so I happen to mention that I might like to go into pre-law. She looked at me like I said I wanna see her with her pants down. She said someone with my athletic potential shouldn't be tryin' to make his college career too complicated. She said, "Why don't you major in P.E., enjoy your college years, then maybe come back here in a few years and teach gym?" She said pre-law was too demandin' and that I couldn't afford to miss all those classes while we were on the road playin' basketball, and that my grades would slip and I probably wouldn't get accepted into a law school anyway. Now I have nothin' against gym teachers, but I've always liked "L.A. Law" and even "Perry Mason." But after talking to her, I felt, you know, kinda useless. So what difference does it make if I make good grades or not?

—I think it does make a difference, Andy. Otherwise this would not have bothered you so much. It's like the system is set up so you don't succeed. I know. I've been there.

—Yeah, man. But you survived.

—So can you, Andy.

—I never liked school all that much anyway. I like gym and I like lunch and I even like history, but don't tell my history teacher that. I got her fooled. She thinks I'm not paying attention, but I could tell her every wife of Henry the Eighth, what he did to each one, and why. But she never asks.

—Why do *you* think she never calls on you?

—I don't know. I guess she just assumes I'm another stupid black kid. So it's easier to pretend to be stupid than to be bothered with all that grade-grubbin' that the white kids do.

Lotsa white kids, and some of the white teachers too, think *all* of us are sorta dumb. They don't say it, but they do. The teachers ask us easier questions, if they ask us anythin' at all, and they expect dumb answers. So I just give 'em what they want.

—What do you think would happen if you *did* volunteer and answer the questions correctly?

—I even tried that. It don't make no difference. Do you know that once I got an A on a test in advanced math, and when the teacher gave back the papers, he said, "Irving got an A, as usual, and Ching Lee got an A, as usual, and, oh my goodness, even *Andy* got an A this week. I must be slipping—my tests are getting too easy if even Andy can get an A on them, or maybe he cheated." Everybody chuckled, but I was boilin' mad. How come I can't ever get praised for good grades? How come me gettin' an A on a test is somethin' the class should laugh at?

—Do you find this frustration from teachers of both races?

—Even some of the black teachers treat us wrong. They be grinnin' in the faces of those little white girls, sayin' stuff like, "That's wonderful, Mary Alice! You did a marvelous job on that project!" Then they say stuff to me like, "That's good, Andy, but couldn't you have improved this part or enhanced this section?" No matter what I do, it's never good enough, so why bother?

—Are good grades important to you, Andy?

—Yeah, I guess.

—Why?

—'Cause good grades makes my father shut up and my mother to smile a lot. She's good at that—smilin'. Just like my dad is good at yellin'.

—What about you? Do *you* care?

—Not really. I just wanna have fun.

—Are you having fun, Andy?

—Not much these days.

—Our time is almost up. Let's get together after the Christmas holidays and talk about how you managed.

—Whatever you say. Look, man, I gotta get goin' anyway. I promised Keisha that I'd go to the mall with her so she can finish her Christmas shoppin'. I don't know what it is with girls and malls.

—Now *that's* a problem I can't help you with.

—And you call yourself a professional!

—Seriously, Andy, I want you to call me at any time if you need me, you hear?

—I hear you. I guess I should say "Merry Christmas."

—Happy holidays to you too, Andy. Take care.

—Peace, man. Later.

FEMALE FRUSTRATION

Keisha's Diary Entry

DECEMBER 17

Dear Diary:

*I just got home from the mall with Andy. It was fun at first. There were at least a million people there, and most of them had kids. We walked around and looked in all the stores, and he asked me what I wanted for Christmas. I told him I wanted to be surprised, but I like perfume. So then we went to the department store and I tried on sixteen different kinds of perfume samples. Man, did I stink good! After a while, we couldn't tell the difference between one smell and another, but we kept spraying samples till the salesladies in the perfume department started asking us to leave. (Where do they **get** those women with that perfect makeup? The only place I've ever seen women with makeup like that* is in the cosmetic area of a big department store. No _real_ woman walks down the street looking like that!)

Anyway, we left there and got something to eat. Then we passed by the Santa Claus display and Andy started acting funny. He said Santa Claus reminded him of Rob. I don't see how. Rob was six feet five and black and I've _never_ seen a tall, skinny black Santa. So Andy started getting depressed and he wouldn't talk and he just wasn't any fun. I called Mom to pick us up. (It sure is a pain since Andy can't drive anymore.) By the time she got there, Andy was just sitting on a bench in the mall, totally ignoring me, with his head down almost on his lap. Mom was pretty cool. She asked Andy if he felt okay, and when he said he had a cold, she took him home. I don't know if she knows how depressed he gets. On the way home from Andy's house, we talked about other things—like taking a shower to get rid of some of that perfume. (In the car, with the heat on, it was starting to make me feel sick.) We stopped by McDonald's and she never said anything else about Andy.

I wonder what Andy's getting me for Christmas. I wonder if Andy is even going to _get_ me anything for Christmas. He's so out of it sometimes that I wonder if he even knows what day it is. All I know is, he better get me something nice, because I spent _too_ much of my baby-sitting money on that sweater I got him.

"HOW AM I SUPPOSED TO WRITE POETRY?"

Poetry Homework for English Class

DECEMBER 20

POEM OF HOPE

Andy Jackson
Poetry Homework
December 20

It's dark where I am
And I cannot find the light.
There are shadows all around me
And my heart is full of fright.

Everyone is cheerful.
They never even see
That storm clouds are forming
Upon the peaceful sea.

I cannot see the future
And I cannot change the past
But the present is so heavy
I don't think I'm going to last.

—Class, pass your papers up. I know you're excited because this is the last day of school before Christmas vacation, but let's get this one last assignment in. At least you know what I'll be doing over the break—reading your poetry. I'm really rather looking forward to it.

—Yeah, just like an English teacher— poetry turns her on.

—Don't knock it till you've tried it, Gerald. Poetry is a wonderful way to express yourself. Sometimes a poem can say what we're able to feel, but unable to put into words ourselves. You like music, don't you?

—Yeah, 'cause it has a live bass and I can turn it up loud and jam.

—Do the songs that you listen to have words?

—Yeah, 'specially rap songs.

—Well, believe it or not, the words to those songs are poetry. Someone has written a poem, and a musician has set that poem to music with a beat. That's all poetry is. Poetry is a song without music. Can you deal with that?

—Yeah, but I still like what I hear on the radio better than what they put in this poetry book.

—That's my point exactly. If you don't like these, write your own! Now do I have all the papers? Andy, where's yours?

—I didn't do it.

—Oh, Andy, why not? This was the last big grade for this quarter. You've missed quite a bit of homework the past few weeks. I know you haven't felt well, but this was an easy assignment.

—Yeah, well, I forgot. I'm sorry.

—I am too, Andy. I hope you have a great vacation. Come back in January and let's start fresh, all right?

—I can live with that.

—Well, there's the bell—I wish you all a very Merry Christmas.

—Hey, Andy, I thought you did that poetry assignment.

—I did. It's in my book bag.

—So why didn't you turn it in? That's going to fry you when grades come out.

—I know. I don't even care. I just didn't feel like it, okay, Keisha?

—Okay, okay. Don't get all bent out of shape. Are you still coming over tonight?

—Yeah, I'll be there. That's one thing that I *do* care about.

Love is special,
Love is fine,
It sends warm shimmers
Down my spine.

His touch is like
    caressing fire.
His smile can make me
    feel desire.

His eyes are kind,
His arms are strong,
I've found the place
    where I belong.

What's your problem, little man?
Can't you deal with the basic plan?
Your mama don't know
And your daddy don't know
That you got a secret
And it's going to blow.

What's your secret, little man?
Can't you hide it under the sand?
Your brother don't know
And your buddy don't know
That you got a problem
And it won't let go.

What's your problem, little man?
Can't you deal with the basic plan?
Your mama don't know
And your daddy don't know
That you got a secret
And it's going to blow.

B. J. Carson
Poetry Homework
December 20

I pray to the Lord
Who lives up above
To send me a lady—
Someone to love.

She's got to be fine,
Of the beautiful sort,
And Lord, if You can—
She's got to be short.

She's got to have class
And a sweet sort of grace,
And she's got to light up
When she sees my face.

She'd care about others
With a little bit of style
And she'd go to her church
Every once in a while.

I know You're real busy
So I'm not asking much.
Just a sweet little lady
That warms to my touch.

MY teacher said to write
A poem about some stuff.
I really don't like poetry
And I think I've had enough.

The words are all arranged
In a funny sort of way
That you cannot understand
If you try and try all day.

There's poems about the flowers
And poems about the trees.
I think that I'd go crazy
If I tried to write like these.

She said listen to my music
But *my* music makes good sense.
'Cause rappers speak in street talk
And are never hard or dense.

So I'm going to tell my teacher
That I'm not going to fight it,
I did my best with poetry
But I just couldn't write it.

Dear Ms. Blackwell,

　　I know this is a little late. I thought about what you said in class, but this is all I could come up with in study hall. Do I get points for trying? Have a good Christmas!

　　　　　　　　　　　Gerald

CHRISTMAS WITHOUT ROB

Andy and the Psychologist

DECEMBER 29

—I'm glad you came back, Andy. I'd like to
finish our conversation.

—What conversation? I do all the talkin'.
All you do is sit there and look out the window.
You know, you really should trim those nose
hairs.

—Thanks for the cosmetic advice. Now,
what about you? We never really talked about
Keisha, or Christmas, or the rest of the
school year up to this point. Do you feel
ready to get started?

—Yeah, I guess. Let me see . . . Christmas . . .
Well, Christmas was kinda rough. Me and
Rob used to hang out in the malls during the
holidays, checkin' out stuff that cost too
much and pretendin' to be interested in

buyin' it. It was funny—we would walk into one of those stores with alarms and bells and electronic wires on the leather goods—you know the type I mean.

—Yes, I'm with you.

—The salespeople started to follow you around as soon as you hit the door, and they *never* take their eyes off you, like you gonna steal somethin' with the Bells of St. Mary's connected to it. Now, white boys can go in there, and when they say, "Just browsing," the salespeople leave 'em alone. Sure, they watch 'em, but they relax a little and stay behind the counter. But let a black dude walk through the door, and it's "Security Alert" in the first degree.

—You're right. I've had it happen to me.

—So then we would say, talkin' real properlike, "My partner and I are interested in purchasing one of your more expensive commodities. Would you be so kind as to allow me to try on this leather coat?" The saleslady, who was always some white lady with too much perfume and too much makeup, would get real nervous and start lookin' toward the back room, where I guess her boss or some security guy was. (And don't let all four of us come in together—the old biddy would just about wet her pants!) But she *had* to let us try it on, 'cause there was the chance that we really did have $5,000 in our back pockets. After all, we're drug dealers anyway, right? Isn't that what they think?

—You know, at this point, I'm supposed to say, "Now Andy, let's not exaggerate here." But what you're describing happens all the time. How does that make you feel?

—Same way it makes you feel—like cheap crap. So, anyway, we'd play with her for a while, then tell her we'd be right back with Daddy's credit card. I know they thought we were scopin' them for a robbery—if you look back into the store right after we left, you could see her writin' down vital information, scribblin' furiously our height and weight and skin color so she can identify us when we come back to rob her silly behind. We would laugh and go on to another store, but it really made me kinda mad that they treated us that way.

—Did all of you feel anger at these kinds of incidents?

—Yeah. It made us wanna break somethin' or hurt somebody. We never did, but I can see how places get mobbed or looted if folks get mad enough. Sometimes you get sick of bein' treated like dirt.

—I hear you. So what else did you fellas do in the mall?

—Well, then we'd go to sit on Santa Claus's lap and get our pictures taken. Just when they were about to snap the picture (and they'll take a picture of *anybody* who'll give them the

$8.95), we'd pull down his beard, or take off his hat, or say real loud, "Why, you're not Santa—you're just some old white dude!" He'd get really mad, but since there was always a bunch of little kids in line, he'd smile and say, "Santa doesn't like bad little boys—you guys run along now." We'd jump up and leave before they had a chance to call Security. I never could figure out why any black kid would want to sit on the lap of some old stinky-breath white man in a red suit and tell him what he wanted for Christmas anyway. How come stores never have black Santa Clauses?

—I don't know, Andy. I used to wonder the same thing.

—So Christmas was rough this year. The malls seemed so phony—all that glitter and shiny stuff—giant green balls and red ribbons hung from the ceiling, with signs like, The Magic of the Season Is at Midtowne Mall. All they care about is how much money you got in your pocket or what the limit is on your credit card. And if you ain't got no money or no credit card, you can just pass up the Magic Midtowne Mall, 'cause we're takin' up a parkin' space from payin' customers.

—Very cynical observation, but probably true. Didn't you go to the mall with Keisha recently? How'd that go?

—Well, it was about two weeks ago. When I went with Keisha to the mall, and when I saw the

Santa Claus display, I got *real* depressed. I had to go home. It just brought back too many memories. Keisha understood, though. She's okay.

—Does she have any problem with helping you with your emotional ups and downs?

—Naw, Keisha's cool. If it hadn't been for Keisha, I mighta really gotten depressed. After the accident, Keisha was always there. She came to the hospital, to the funeral, to the trial. She was the only one I could cry in front of and not be embarrassed. My father kept telling me to put it behind me, to quit dwellin' on the past, to get on with my life, but Keisha said stuff like, "I know it hurts, baby—go ahead and let it out." Sometimes we'd be sittin' on the couch in her livin' room, and she would hold me and I would cry so hard my whole body would shake, and then I'd fall asleep with my head on her lap. Me and her never really—you know—did it—I think I like her too much to do that right now. I talk big in front of the boys, but they know Keisha's special to me.

—Do you depend a lot on Keisha?

—Yeah, I guess so. She's there for me when nobody else is.

—Suppose Keisha wasn't there? What would you do?

—No chance, man. Me and Keisha are tight. She's my lady.

—Relationships end all the time. Could

you take it if you had another serious personal loss?

—Naw, man. You don't understand. Look,
let me give you an example. It was Christmas
Day. I gave Keisha a bottle of that perfume
that she wanted and she gave me a real nice
sweater. Everything was cool. We were sittin'
in my livin' room. Our Christmas tree was all
shiny and glowin'. My dad was dozin' in his
chair, Mama was workin' a puzzle that I had
given her (she likes word puzzles), and Monty
was playin' with some space soldier people
that he got for Christmas. I felt—I don't
know—sorta "at peace." If that one moment
coulda continued forever, life would be sweet.

—But it didn't.

—No. The phone rang and spoiled it all. It
was Rob's mother. She was all teary-soundin'
and she said she just wanted to wish me a
Merry Christmas. See, she used to call me
every Christmas and tell me to come and pick
up my rock. It was this silly joke-thing we did
every year.

—Your rock? I don't understand.

—You know how they say that kids who
are bad won't get any Christmas presents and
will only get a rock in their stockin'? Well,
every year, she'd call me up and tell me to
come and get my rock. Then I'd say, "But I
been good!" So then she'd say, "Well, if that's
the case, come on over and let's see what else

we can find for you." I'd go over later and she'd always have somethin' cool like a Lakers hat or a Bulls T-shirt for me.

—So this year, did she mention the rock?

—No. I think she wanted to. But neither one of us could get past that part about whether I been good or not. It upset the both of us. She hung up real quick. I think she was sorry she called.

—Were you sorry that she called?

—Yeah, I was. It spoiled that one special moment of peace and it made me start thinkin' 'bout all the pain in my life. Keisha could tell somethin' was wrong, but she didn't ask. She leaned her head on my shoulder and started singin' "Silent Night" real quietly.

—Did that make you feel better?

—Yeah. I relaxed a little. Then my dad woke up, and I guess he thought things were gettin' too cozy, 'cause he said it was gettin' late and I probably should be walkin' Keisha home.

—So you feel secure in your relationship?

—Yeah, man. Me and Keisha are tight. She keeps me on balance. When my parents get on my last nerve, or school gets to be too much, or I get really depressed, I can call her and she'll cheer me up. She believes in me. That means a lot.

—Well, Andy, I really enjoy these sessions with you. Would you be willing to come back again? Perhaps we need to discuss some aspects of your life just a little more. And once you get started, you don't really seem to mind, am I right?

—I guess not. It does kinda help to talk about some of this stuff.

—Good. See you next time.

—Later, man.

"GOOD MORNING, HAZELWOOD"

Morning Announcements First Day Back after Christmas Vacation

JANUARY 7

DING. DONG. DING.
—*Good morning, Hazelwood. May I have your attention, please? These are the morning announcements for Monday, January 7. Would you all please rise for the saying of the Pledge of Allegiance?*

    —I pledge allegiance to the flag of the United States of America and to the republic for which it stands, one nation under God, indivisible, with liberty and justice for all.

    —*Welcome back from Christmas vacation. We hope you had a safe and restful holiday and have come back ready with a positive attitude to successfully handle the academic tasks before you.*
    —*The Unity Cultural Association wishes to*

thank all students who brought in canned goods for needy families. We were able to donate over thirty baskets of food to area families. Thank you for your support, and thank you especially to Room 225 for bringing in exactly 225 cans. Please contact the U.C.A. to schedule your pizza party.

—The SAT scores have arrived and are available to be picked up in the Senior High Counseling Office. If you would like to discuss your scores, please make an appointment with the secretary there to see your counselor. Also, a reminder to juniors that college plan forms are due in the next thirty days.

—Tryouts will be held next week for the annual Hazelwood Talent Show. If you can sing, or dance, or tell jokes, get your act together and get ready to show your stuff! More details to follow.

—The Hazelwood Tigers Basketball Team won Friday against Taylorville, by a score of 88-56. That's the sixth Tiger victory in a row. Captain Andy Jackson and forward Tyrone Mills led the team with twenty points each. Our Tigers meet the Erieview Eagles this Friday. Tickets will be on sale every day during lunch.

—All girls interested in running for the championship Lady Tigers Track Team should sign up in the gym office. Indoor practice starts soon.

—This concludes the morning announcements. Have a pleasant day.

DING. DONG. DING.

BLACK ON WHITE

Andy and Keisha
on a Snowy Day

JANUARY 11

—Hello, may I speak to Andy? . . . Hi, Andy, this is Keisha. Have you looked outside yet?

—Girl, I ain't even awake good yet. What's up?

—It snowed last night! Must be about six inches out there. And it's still coming down hard.

—Shucks. I hate snow. It gets all in my shoes and I walk 'round with cold, wet toes all day.

—So wear some boots.

—You sound like my mama.

—And you sound like a two-year-old. I just wanted to let you know about the snow. Get up and get going. Your dad'll probably have you shoveling.

—You got that right. You think they'll cancel school?

—Be for real! They *never* close the city schools. The lucky ones are the kids who live in places like Boone County—out in the country. They always get off school in the winter.

—Yeah, no such luck for us. I'll see you at school, wet feet and all.

—Ain't nobody even here. I shoulda stayed home. I hate snow.

—Oh, Andy, you complain too much. It's so pretty. Look how shiny and glistening everything looks. The trees, even the telephone lines, all look different—like they've been decorated.

—You a trip, Keisha. You always see the bright side of everythin'.

—What can I say? I'm a rose in the snow— the bright spot in your dark, seems-like-it's-always-depressed life.

—You got that right. There's the bell. Let's get to class. Think Ms. Blackwell is absent?

—Not a chance.

—Yeah, she's a fire-breathin' dragon. All she got to do is breathe hard and the snow in front of her'll melt!

—Oh, Andy, she's not so bad.

—That woman and her poetry are gonna drive me crazy!

—Well, since we have so many absences because of the snow, we'll have an easy day.

—Now you talkin', Ms. Blackwell.

—I have a poem I'd like to share with you.

—See, I *told* you. The woman be *trippin'* on poetry!

—I heard that, Andy. Try this one and see if you like it. It's called "One Thousand Nine Hundred and Sixty-Eight Winters," by Jacqueline Earley.

Got up this morning
Feeling good and black
Thinking black thoughts
Did black things
Played all my black records
And minded my own black business
Put on my best black clothes
Walked out my black door
And, Lord have mercy: white snow!

—Hey, that's funny. You right, Ms. Blackwell—that one's not so bad. That's exactly how I felt this morning when I saw all that snow outside.

—Thanks, Andy. Coming from you, that's a real compliment. Gerald, what do you think?

—Hey, that's the way I feel *every* day. Sometimes I just feel like there's white everywhere I look, you know what I mean?

—Not exactly.

—It's like the snow today—like you go outside and there's white all around you—like swallowing you up.

—Go on.

—Like the lady said in the poem—you mindin' your own black business and all this white stuff jus' takes over your life. And I ain't jus' talkin' 'bout snow!

—What's wrong with white, Gerald?

—Nothin', Mary Alice. This ain't no personal thing 'bout you or any other white person. I'm just tryin' to explain a feelin' I got.

—That shows a real depth of understanding, Gerald—of the poem, and of some of the larger ideas that the poem touches on. I'm glad you liked the poem. What did *you* think, Mary Alice?

—I never really thought about it. But I guess Gerald is right. Sometimes it must be mind-boggling!

—Good. Any other comments? Keisha?

—I like the poem. All of us at one time or another feel like a cinder among the snowflakes. You stand out when you just want to blend in; you get noticed whether you want to or not. But it's not always racial. In one of my classes, I'm the only girl. That's just as bad.

—Good point, Keisha.

—Ms. Blackwell?

—Yes, Andy?

—Why is it that in literature and poems

and everythin' we read in English class, black usually stands for somethin' bad and white stands for somethin' good? The good guys always ride a white horse, and the bad guy is always a black-hearted villain. How come?

—I'm not sure, Andy, but it certainly is apparent in literature. I don't think it's completely racially motivated, however. The tones of black and white have the greatest amount of contrast between them, therefore writers and poets, who have always dealt with extremes in passion and people, use black and white to create those images of contrast. Can you think of any other example where color is used as a metaphor to express an idea? Or where black is used as a positive and white is used as a negative?

—How about green with envy?

—Yellow fear?

—Icy blue!

—Purple passion!

—Ruby red lips!

—How about white heat?

—Or white as death?

—I know a real weird one. Chocolate is dark, right?

—Right! Brown and luscious!

—Ever eat white chocolate? It's even better!

—Dag! Everything good that's dark, they take it and make it white!

—How about black magic! Is that better than white magic?

—It's more powerful!

—Well then, what about black gold? Oil! I'd be rich!

—Excellent, class. As you have shown, color is used all the time to create images in our mind. It's society that implants positives or negatives onto certain ideas. You have the option to accept, reject, or change the stereotypes that currently exist.

—How do you mean?

—Okay, let me give you an example. In Puritan England, about 300 years ago, it was against the law to wear the color red. Anyone caught wearing red would be arrested and probably killed.

—Why? That's stupid.

—It wasn't stupid to them. They associated red with the devil and works of evil; therefore, anyone who wore that color must be guilty of evildoing.

—Hey, Keisha! You better get rid of that red sweater you're wearin'! I heard a police car go by. I'd be glad to hold it for you.

—Shut up, Gerald. You are just used to running from police cars!

—Okay, now, calm down. Let me give you another example of how color bias can be changed—and this one *is* racial in nature. About twenty to twenty-five years ago, social activists started a campaign to get rid of unfair, negative racial stereotypes. That's when we first started hearing the phrases, "Black is beautiful" and "Say it loud, I'm black and I'm proud!" Before that, black people in America had been called all sorts of terrible names. And all those thousands of years of the Black Knight and black cats and the blackness of death that people associated with negative ideas were associated with a group of people whose skin happened to be darker than the skin of the folks who seemed to be in charge here. Even Africa was called "the Dark Continent."

—I see what you mean. My mother told me about all that stuff. She said when she was little, all she could buy were white dolls. Every little black girl had a beautiful white baby doll with long blonde curls to love and to hug.

—You're right, Rhonda. I had one like that myself.

—You did? Now *that's* funny!

—Well, times have changed. Stereotypes of color, race, and gender are slowly disappearing. It's up to you people to make a world that is better. Well, there's the bell. Good discussion, class. No homework tonight. Enjoy the snow.

—Are your feet cold, Andy?

—Not really. Yeah, maybe a little. Hey, Keisha, can I ask you somethin'?

—Sure.

—Do you think Robbie is cold?

—What?

—It's so cold today. And there's so much snow. Do you think he's cold?

—What makes you think of stuff like that?

—I was just thinkin' about how cold my feet are and how uncomfortable it makes me feel. And I was just wonderin' if Robbie is feeling like this all over.

—Andy, I don't think you should be talking like this.

—So cold. So cold. I can't stand it! I can't stop thinkin' 'bout Robbie out there frozen and cold in the cemetery. It's drivin' me crazy!

—Andy, stop it! You're driving *me* crazy. Robbie can't feel anything, Andy. Robbie is warm and at peace.

—Are you sure?

—As sure as I can be.

—Warm?

—Warm.

—At peace?

—At peace. Like I wish *you* could be. Now let's get out of here. If we miss the bus and have to walk in all this snow, then we'll *really* know what cold is.

—Okay, okay. Here I come. . . . Cold. . . . Cold. . . . So cold. . . .

ACCEPTING FEAR— ESCAPING PAIN

Andy and the Psychologist

JANUARY 12

—So Andy, here we are again. Are you ready?

—You called the meetin', boss.

—How do you like all this cold weather?

—I don't. Everything is cold and dirty and generally depressin'.

—Do you find yourself depressed very often?

—Yeah, sometimes I don't even want to get out of bed.

—Do you feel sad?

—Not really. Just heavy, like I'm carryin' 'round Mike Tyson's punchin' bag inside of me.

—Do you ever feel like you're "out of touch" with reality?

—Well, yeah, now that you mention it. Me and Keisha went for a long walk a couple of weeks ago (I have no wheels anymore—remember?). We'd been talkin' 'bout Rob and the holidays and how his family must have felt.

—Have you talked to either of Rob's parents since that phone call you had from his mother on Christmas Day?

—Naw, man. I ain't got the nerve. I know they must hate me. Why would they want to talk to the person who killed their son?

—It might be worth a try. You were Rob's best friend, weren't you?

—Yeah, I guess.

—I bet they'd be glad to talk to you.

—Maybe.

—So go ahead—you were talking about the walk you took with Keisha.

—Yeah. We stopped at a freeway overpass, and we just stood there for a minute, watchin' the cars whiz under us. Their lights were on, and they came at us like bullets, it seemed—too fast to count. I thought about the four of us the night of the accident, on that same expressway, and I noticed that the retainin' wall was really only 'bout four feet high.

—Did you remember it differently?

—Yeah. That night, it seemed like a mountain. And the longer I stood there, the more I became like—sorta hypnotized by the slick whistlin' of the cars as they rushed beneath us. And I wanted to jump.

90

—Why do you think you felt like that?

—I don't know why—I just felt like I should be down there, like if I were part of that fast-movin' rush, I wouldn't *feel* anythin' anymore, and everythin' would be cool again. I think I even leaned over, really ready to join those bullet-things down below.

—So what happened then?

—Keisha grabbed my jacket and screamed at me, "Andy Jackson! Get your stupid butt away from that railing! Are you crazy?" It's like I sorta came to then, and I looked at her as if she was from another planet. I guess I was the one actin' spacey, but she just told me to take her home. By the time we got to her house, it had started to snow, and we were both breathin' normally again.

—Did she say anything else?

—No. I just looked at her, and I said, like real soft and easy—"Thanks." Then I kissed her real lightly on the lips and went home. We never mentioned it again. And nothin' like that ever happened again.

—Why did you say you felt like you should be down there with the cars? Did you feel like you wanted to die?

—Die? . . . Yeah. . . . No. . . . I don't know. Why you talkin' 'bout dyin'?

—Have you ever thought about being dead, Andy?

—I used to. Right after the accident I

91

wanted to be dead. I wanted it to be me that was dead instead of Rob. I wanted the hurtin' to go away.

—What about now? Do you ever think about death?

—To tell you the truth, man, I think about it all the time.

—Does that frighten you?

—Yeah, sometimes. It seems like bein' dead is the only way I'll ever feel alive again. Does that make sense?

—Sure it does, Andy. You're hurting and you can't find an escape from the pain and you're frightened because the only way out seems to be something you can't even verbalize. Am I right?

—Yeah, man. You're the first person that will even talk about death to me. People are scared of it, and nobody, not even my friends and family, wants to talk about it. It's kinda a relief to bring it out finally.

—There's nothing wrong with thinking about or talking about death, Andy. And it's normal for your thoughts to center on this subject. After all, the death of a friend is a traumatic experience in itself.

—So I ain't crazy?

—Not even a little bit.

—Suppose it's more than just thinkin' about death in general. Suppose I told you I sometimes think about killin' myself.

—I'd say I'm not surprised. Sometimes it's part of the guilt and grieving process—to consider suicide as an alternative to the pain. But the answer is *life,* Andy, not death. So then I'd tell you about the other alternatives to help eliminate the pain.

—Like what?

—Like talking to Rob's parents. Like writing a letter to Rob. Like talking to other kids who might consider drinking and driving. Do you think you could handle any of those?

—Yeah, probably. Maybe. I don't really know.

—And then I'd ask you to promise me that if you got so depressed that you didn't think you could handle the situation, you'd call me before you did anything to harm yourself. Could you promise that?

—Yeah, I'd call you. But I ain't stupid, man. I might think about it, I might even threaten it, but I ain't hardly gonna kill myself. I ain't got the nerve.

—That's good. Do you feel a little better now that we've verbalized some things that you were unsure of or unwilling to talk about?

—Yeah, I do.

—Do you think if you wrote a letter to Rob, or to his parents, it would help eliminate some of the pain?

—I don't know. I never thought about it.

—Why don't you try to write one of those

letters and bring it next time that you come, okay?

—Dag! Now I got homework from my shrink! I can't win.

—Yes, you can, Andy. You're a winner all the way.

—You really think so?

—I know so. You remember now—you promise to call me if you need me—any time of the day or night, okay?

—Yeah, okay.

—Peace, man.

—Later.

NIGHT AND DREAMS

Andy and Monty
Just before Bedtime

JANUARY 14

—Hey, Andy—would you turn my light back on?

—Why? You scared of the dark, Monty?

—No, I just want to be able to see stuff while I'm fallin' asleep.

—How you gonna see stuff? Your eyes be closed.

—Yeah, but if I hafta open 'em real quick—like if it was a fire or a robber or a monster or something—I could see what I needed to see.

—Okay, okay, I'll leave the light on. You get to sleep now.

—Andy?

—What?

—When you dream, do you dream in color or in black and white?

—I don't know. I never thought about it. Where do you get these questions?

—Hey, I'm six years old. I got a lot to learn.

—You got that right.

—So, tell me. Are dreams in color, like on TV, or black and white, like those old movies that Daddy likes to watch?

—I guess dreams are in color. That makes sense, don't it?

—Maybe black people dream in color, and white people dream in black and white. That makes sense to me.

—Seems to me that stuff that makes sense to you don't make much sense to nobody else in the world. Who knows? You may be right. Now go to sleep.

—Andy?

—What?

—Do you ever have bad dreams?

—Yeah, man. Sometimes. I guess everybody does at one time or another.

—About monsters and robbers and stuff?

—Naw, man. That's kiddie nightmares. I have grown-up nightmares about chemistry tests and dragon-breathin' teachers and bein' caught in a rich white neighborhood after midnight.

—That ain't scary.

—It's scary if you're seventeen. Let's get some sleep now. You ask too many questions.

—Are you gonna go to sleep now too?

—Yeah, in a little bit. I'm gonna call Keisha and then I'll turn in.

—When'll Mama and Daddy be home?

—I don't know. They went out to dinner—first time in a long time. They need to get out every once in a while.

—Yeah, I guess. I'm not scared, though, 'cause I got my light on, and I got you in the next room.

—Oh, wow! You got Andy the Mighty Protector!

—Yeah, and if that don't work, I got my Teenage Warrior Space Soldier.

—You sleep with that thing?

—Yeah, why not?

—You too big to be sleepin' with stuff like that.

—I am not. If *you* slept with a warrior space soldier, maybe you wouldn't have nightmares either.

—I'll keep that in mind. Good night, little dude.

—Good night, Andy.

—Hello, may I speak to Keisha? . . . Hi, Keisha. Watcha doin'?

—Nothing much. Finishing up my homework and thinking about you.

—Oh yeah? Good stuff?

—Yeah, mostly.

—Like what?

—Like how much fun you can be sometimes. Like how patient you are with Monty.
Like how things brighten up when you're
smiling.

—You ever think bad stuff about me?

—Sometimes. I mean, sometimes I worry
about you.

—Yeah, I know. Sometimes I worry about
myself.

—How come?

—Like for instance, I look at Monty and
his future looks so bright. He's cute and he's
smart. He'll be a doctor or a lawyer some day.
I can tell. But me, I don't see me bein' nothin'
in the future.

—You mean you see yourself as one of
those street people with no place to go?

—No. I mean I don't see myself at all.
When I think about the future, all I see is a
blank—and darkness.

—That's depressing. What do you see for
me in the future?

—You? You gonna be the first black
woman somethin'-or-other. If there ain't one
yet, you gonna be it.

—You're crazy. And don't you see yourself with me as the husband (or maybe the
secret lover) of the first black woman some-
thing-or-other?

—No, I don't. I don't know where I'll be, but I'm not there with you. I'm not anywhere.

—Very strange, your visions of the future. What about the near future, like next Friday?

—That far, I can see.

—Do you see us getting together?

—I see us at a movie. . . . I see us at Mickey D's for burgers. . . . I see us makin' passionate love in the moonlight!

—I think your crystal ball is cracked. But two out of three ain't bad.

—Which two were right?

—Get off the phone, silly dude. I'll see you tomorrow.

—G'night, Keisha. You know, I like talkin' to you on the phone.

—Why?

—'Cause you don't make fun of me when I start talkin' off-the-wall stuff. And you listen to whatever foolishness I got to say.

—That's 'cause I like you, Andy. And I care about you.

—You're somethin' special, you know.

—That's what all the fellas say.

—Girl, get outta here. Talk to you tomorrow.

—Okay, Andy. Bye. You going to sleep now?

—Yeah. My head is on the pillow and I'm gonna fall asleep thinkin' 'bout you.

—Then I guess you'll have sweet dreams. Good night.

—'Night, Keisha.

—Andy! Andy! Andy! Why are you sleepin' in that soft warm bed with the fresh blue pillowcases? I'm cold, Andy. Can I borrow a blanket?

—Who's there? Who said that?

—It's me, brother. Your main man, Roberto. And yes, I'm cold. Very cold. It's no fun bein' dead.

—I'm sorry, Rob. You know I didn't mean to hurt you.

—Understood, my man. But when're you comin' to keep me company?

—Me?

—We could play some one-on-one. You know I always could beat you.

—What you talkin' about? You want me to be dead?

—Yeah, man, with you dead, it'll be live! Wait a minute. Does that make sense?

—None of this makes sense. What do you want, Robbie?

—I want *you,* Andy. You. Ain't no black folks in the part of Heaven that I been assigned to and I'm bored.

—What?

—Computer foul-up. Since my last name

is Washington, they put me in the section with George and Martha. Nice folks, but boring! George never even heard of basketball, and Martha keeps askin' why there ain't no slave quarters in Heaven. So I spend most of my time (which, by the way, is an eternity) bringin' 'em up to date on American history. And you *know* I slept through most of Killian's class, so I'm runnin' out of things to tell 'em.

—Rob, you drivin' me crazy! None of this makes any sense. I must be dreamin'!

—Sure, you're dreamin'. You know, if you had a Teenage Warrior Space Soldier with you, I couldn't be botherin' you. They're pretty powerful, you know.

—You mean Monty was right?

—Sure. And tell him he's also right about dreams. It's true—black folks do dream in color. Big dreams need technicolor. So, when you comin'?

—I can't, Rob. Please leave me alone.

—It's all your fault, you know. All your fault. You got the beer. You drove the car. You smashed into the wall. You killed me. And now you gotta come and keep me company.

—No! I swear I didn't mean to! It was an accident! A horrible, horrible accident!

—I'm waitin' for ya, Andy. . . . I'm waiting. . . .

—No! No! No! Get outta here! Leave me alone!

—Andy? You okay?

—Wha—? What? Whatsa matter, Monty? Why you in here?

—You were screamin'. Did you have a bad dream after all?

—A bad dream? Yeah, I guess so. I'm okay now.

—You want my Teenage Warrior Space Soldier? I got two. Rocketman is the most powerful, but Astroman has the most weapons.

—Hey, just to make you happy, I'm gonna take Rocketman, okay? Now go back to bed. I'm sorry I woke you up.

—G'nite, Andy.

—G'nite, Monty. And thanks.

A LETTER OF REMEMBERED JOY

Andy's Letter to Rob's Parents

JANUARY 18

Dear Mr. and Mrs. Washington,

If I stood on my head and stripped butt-naked in the middle of Fountain Square, screamin "I'M SORRY!" as loud as I could, it still wouldn't be enough. How can you tell the parents of your best friend that you're sorry that you killed their son? There's no words to cover something that awful. I know you must hate me. I wish there was some way I could've traded places with him, you know, like I should have died, and Rob should be okay.

I dreamed about Rob a couple of nights ago. It made me start to thinking about stuff we used to do together. So, instead of writing, "I'm sorry about what happened" 6,000 times on a sheet of notebook paper (like the teachers used to make us do in elementary school when we were bad), I decided to write you this letter to help you remember the good stuff, instead of the bad. I hope this gives you some comfort, and I hope one day you can start to forgive me.

These are my memories of Rob:

I REMEMBER—

—Spending the night at your house, and staying up all night watching cable, eating the pizza that we ordered at 3:00 a.m.

—Going for ice cream after practice, even though you always said you weren't going to stop, but you always did.

—Playing basketball with a rolled-up sock and a wastebasket in Rob's bedroom, ignoring you and laughing when you said to cut out all that noise.

—Finishing off two extra-large boxes of frosted flakes with ease during those small after-school "snacks."

—Riding in the backseat of your station wagon, all dressed up and nervous, the night me and Rob double-dated for the Freshman Dance, and you had to drive us because we didn't have our licenses yet.

—Sitting in your backyard in the summer, eating Bar-B-Q, and listening to stories from Rob's granpa about "down home."

—Going to King's Island with you on family discount day and riding The Beast 47 times in a row.

—Driving backward through the drive-through at McDonald's, and getting in trouble and having to call you, not for driving backward, but because we were so busy being silly, we forgot we didn't have enough money to pay for the hamburgers.

—Getting chicken pox, both of us, in the eighth grade, and staying at your house for a week, because we couldn't go to school.

—Eating spaghetti at your house on Saturday night and having "worm-slurping" contests to see who could suck the longest piece of spaghetti.

—Seeing you in the stands during all our basketball games, knowing that you'd always be there, and feeling good about that, even if we lost.

—Wishing that I could be a part of your family because you seemed to have something that my family didn't.

These are some of the things I remember about you, your family, and Rob. I will always treasure those days, and I will never forgive myself for destroying something very special. I hope that someday you will be able to forgive me, but if not, I hope you will be able to remember without so much pain.

Yours,
Andy

"OUT, OUT! BRIEF CANDLE!"

Macbeth Lesson
in English Class

JANUARY 21

—All right, class. We've almost finished our study of *Macbeth*. We've watched Macbeth change from a noble, trusted, dedicated soldier, willing to sacrifice his life for king and country, to a wretched, depraved, corrupt murderer who no longer has feelings of guilt or morality. It's a fascinating study of the degeneration of the human spirit.

—Ms. Blackwell, does he die at the end?

—Well, Marcus, he's just about dead inside already. He's got one little spark left—his refusal to surrender to Macduff and the forces of good—but don't you think his death is inevitable, Marcus?

—Yeah, he deserves to die—he killed his best friend, he killed women and children, he killed the king. Yeah, I'd say my man deserves to die.

—Okay, what about his wife? Does she deserve to die too? Mary Alice?

—Well, it *was* originally her idea. If it hadn't been for her, Macbeth never would have killed the king in the first place. Women have that power over men, you know. Right, Keisha?

—Right on, girl. Now you're talking!

—Ooh—You wish! You livin' in "la-la land," ladies!

—Okay, Gerald, that will be enough. Keisha and Mary Alice have a right to their opinions too, you know. But Lady Macbeth, who seemed so strong at the beginning of the play, had a rather rapid mental deterioration—remember she was walking and talking in her sleep and washing her hands uncontrollably? She finally cannot stand the pressure of the guilt, and she kills herself.

—Kills herself? What a wimp! I'm disappointed. I thought she was pretty cool for a while there.

—Sorry, Keisha. She takes the coward's way out by committing suicide and leaves Macbeth to face the end alone. But you must remember that she *was* a murderer. I don't think Shakespeare meant for her to be a hero. That's where we'll start today—where Macbeth learns of his wife's death. Open to page 224—Act 5, Scene 5, line 16. Anthony, would you read, please?

The Queen, my Lord, is dead.

She should have died hereafter;
There would have been a time for such a word.
To-morrow, and to-morrow, and to-morrow,
Creeps in this petty pace from day to day,
To the last syllable of recorded time;
And all our yesterdays have lighted fools
The way to dusty death. Out, out, brief candle!
Life's but a walking shadow, a poor player,
That struts and frets his hour upon the stage,
and then is heard no more. It is a tale
Told by an idiot, full of sound and fury,
Signifying nothing.

—Now let's see what Shakespeare is talking about here. What is he saying about life? B. J.?

—He says, "Life is short, and then you die. And on top of that, life don't really mean nothin' anyway." But I think the only reason that he was so depressed was because he had been the cause of so much death that he couldn't find nothin' else good about livin'.

—That's a wonderful observation, B. J.

See, Shakespeare isn't so bad. You're doing a great job of figuring out what's going on. Andy, what do *you* think about these lines? . . . Andy . . . where are you going? What's wrong? Someone go check on him, please. He seemed pretty upset. Keisha? Tyrone? Go out in the hall and make sure he's all right.

—Okay, class. Let's go on.

BALONEY SANDWICHES AND BAD BREATH

Lunch, and a Visit to the Counselor

FEBRUARY 4

—Hey, B. J. Whatsup? Whatcha got for lunch?

—Nothin' much, Tyronio. Probably baloney again. I *hate* baloney sandwiches.

—Don't you make your own lunch? My mama told me a long time ago, "Tyrone, if you want lunch, you better make it yourself, 'cause I got more important things to do!"

—Naw, man. My mama *loves* me—she takes the time each mornin' to make me a nutritious, delicious luncheon!

—Yeah, baloney sandwiches!! . . . Hey, Andy. Put your tray right here. You have to sit downwind of B. J. He's got baloney and mustard again. Where's Keisha?

—She went to the library to get a book for a report she's got to do. She'll be down in a minute. Tyrone, where's Rhonda?

—She's got a chemistry lab to finish. I do admire intelligent women. Say, Andy, remember when Rob was tryin' to go with that exchange student from Hong Kong because she was so good in math? Remember how she . . .

—Hey! Leave Rob out of this. He's dead, okay? I get sick and tired of you two always talkin' 'bout Rob! Like you tryin' to bring him back or somethin'! What're you tryin' to do—make sure I don't forget that I'm alive and he's dead? Okay, you've made your point—he's dead! He's dead! He's dead! He's *still* dead! Do you hear me? I'm outta here.

—Man, I don't know how to deal with this. It seems like he ought to be gettin' better, but he's gettin' worse. I still have bad dreams 'bout that night, but I'm learnin' to live with it. Andy keeps freakin' out.

—Yeah, B. J., I know where you comin' from. Maybe we should talk to his parents or somethin'.

—Naw, man. That's like talkin' to this baloney sandwich. Wait a minute, I got an idea. Isn't old lady Thorne always sayin' stuff like we should come and talk to her in the counselor's office if we ever have a problem?

—Yeah, but I can't stand her.

—Me neither, but she's got to know somebody who can give Andy some help. That's her job, ain't it?

—You're right. Let's get over there before the bell rings.

—I certainly am glad that you boys have come expressing your concern for your friend. What seems to be the problem?

—Well, Mrs. Thorne, Andy seems depressed all the time and gets mad at us for no reason. Sometimes he starts cryin'. A couple of weeks ago, he ran out of English class because we were readin' a play about some dead white guy.

—It was *Macbeth,* stupid. Anyway, Andy only seems happy when he's with Keisha or when he's actin' weird. And we didn't know who else to talk to.

—Now it's perfectly understandable that Andrew is having a difficult time adjusting to Robert's death. That was a very traumatic experience—for all of you, I might add. His behavior is really not out of the ordinary— anger, depression, even tears—are all positive signs that he is in the process of working it out. If he *didn't* show any of these signs, then we'd be concerned.

—But . . . but . . . it seems like . . .

—. . . like he needs help or somethin'.

—Well, I probably shouldn't tell you boys this, but he *is* getting some outside counseling. I tell you this in the strictest of confidences, because you seem to be so genuinely concerned. So you boys can relax and be assured that he is getting whatever help he needs.

—Well, thanks, Mrs. Thorne.

—Thank you, boys. Andrew should be proud to have such good friends.

—If she hada called me "boy" one more time, I was gonna smack her!

—When you do, smack her in the mouth—her breath be *kickin'*!

LEARNING TO LIVE

Andy's Final Visit
with the Psychologist

FEBRUARY 5

—Well, Andy, it's been a few weeks since we've talked. How've you been?

—Not bad. No real problems. I'm dealin' with the situation.

—That's good to know. I got the copy of the letter you wrote to Rob's parents. Thanks for sending it to me. That wasn't really necessary, you know.

—Yeah, I know, but I wanted you to know I got my stuff together.

—Did you send the letter to Mr. and Mrs. Washington?

—Yeah, I did. I wasn't goin' to at first. I was scared that it would upset them, but I finally mailed it. I didn't have the nerve to give it to them in person.

—Did they respond?

—Yeah, it kinda surprised me. Rob's mom stopped by our house. She cried, and she hugged me and she said she'd treasure that letter forever. I never will figure out women.

—What about Rob's dad?

—She said he forgives me too, but he's havin' a harder time dealin' with this. I can understand where he's comin' from.

—So what about you, Andy? Did it help you to write the letter?

—Yeah, I guess. I'm sleepin' better and I'm doin' better in school.

—No bad dreams?

—No bad dreams. Honest.

—Do you still blame yourself?

—Yeah, I guess I always will, but I'm learnin' to live with it.

—I think if you had said that you no longer felt guilty, I'd be worried. I see quite a bit of improvement in you, Andy. You have progressed from a state of "wanting to die" to the much more positive outlook of "learning to live." That's encouraging.

—Do I hafta keep comin' here? I ain't nuts. I know what I'm doin'. I got my act together. Whatcha think?

—I tell you what. I think we can cut these sessions to an as-needed basis. I want you to call me if your life starts to get "unbalanced" in any way, or if you have any problems whatsoever, and we'll see what we can do to get things straight. You call me, anytime, night or day, you hear?

—Yeah, I hear you. I'll call. I promise. Thanks, man. Later.

—Peace, Andy.

THE IMPORTANCE
OF FRIENDSHIP

Keisha's English Homework

FEBRUARY 6

Keisha Montgomery
English Homework
February 6
Personal Essay
Topic—The Importance of Friendship

    Without friends, life would be boring,
lonely, and meaningless. Nobody comes to high
school for the teachers—not really. We come to
see our friends, to see what they're wearing, who
they're going with, who they broke up with, and
where they're going this weekend. In between
that, we go to classes.

    Friends make life exciting. A phone call
from a friend on a boring Friday night can
bring a spark to an evening that would have
been spent just watching T.V. Going down-

town alone is no fun. Going downtown with a friend can be an adventure. We sit on Fountain Square and laugh at uptight businessmen, all dressed alike in blue suits and red ties. Alone, it's just another boring trip with no one to talk to.

With no friends to talk to or to go places with, life can be very lonely. It's sad to be alone—wanting to share your thoughts with a friend and having no one there, except maybe your little brother or sister, to be with. Sometimes I feel so alone I just want to cry. That's why I'm thankful that I have a good friend like Rhonda, who always has a strong shoulder for me to cry on.

When the bad times come, like when Robbie died, a friend is the most important thing in the world. Rhonda and I cried together, went to the funeral together, and tried to help the boys involved as much as we could. She and Tyrone are doing fine. I'm having a rough time with Andy. I think it's because he lost his best friend and it's hard for him to get over the guilt and the pain. He once told me that his life had lost its meaning.

Andy has many good friends who care about him. Even though nobody can take Robbie's place, all of us, as friends, can survive the situation.

CONCERN AND DENIAL

Phone Call from Andy's Teacher

FEBRUARY 10

—Hello, Mr. Jackson? This is Ms. Blackwell, Andy's English teacher. I'm calling because I'm concerned about Andy's performance and behavior in class.

—I see. I appreciate your call. What seems to be the problem?

—Well, academically, he's really slipping. He's missed four of the last six homework assignments. One of those was a major writing assignment—an essay on the importance of friendship. He's failed the last two quizzes, and we have a test coming up next week that I'm afraid he won't be ready for.

—You know, Andy never has made the grades that my wife and I expected of him. Every year I get calls from his teachers, saying he's not doing his homework, and he's failing tests. He's too old for me to spank. What do I do?

—I'm not sure what your course of action should be. You know him better than I do—I only see him once a day for fifty minutes. But surely some parental encouragement on your part would be helpful in reminding him that he's really only hurting himself. I believe that Andy has the ability—he just needs the desire to get it together. And as a black teacher, it really bothers me to see bright African-American young men like Andy waste their potential.

—I understand where you're coming from. And I appreciate your concern. Do you know some counselor there told him he'd never make it in pre-law?

—I believe it. Of course, to be perfectly balanced, we have plenty of teachers and counselors who are fair and would bend over backward to help Andy, but lately, even his behavior has been working against him.

—How do you mean?

—Well, he's been doing a lot more "acting out" lately. He's always been a cheerful, good-natured kid, with very few inhibitions, which sometimes does not lead to the best classroom behavior. Let's face it. That's teacher talk for: Andy will stand up on a table and sing "God Bless America" at the top of his lungs if he's giving a report on patriotism. The kids love it, and most of the times the teachers at least tolerate it. But lately, he's been doing mean, even dangerous things. For instance, last week he shot a bottle rocket out of a teacher's window, and yesterday he was sent out of my room for spitting on the floor; he was sent out of another class during a test. Andy ripped up a student's test paper and threw it in the trash—*before* the student had even finished the test and turned it in. There seem to be more of these kinds of incidents lately, not at all like the Andy we know and care about.

—I heard about the bottle-rocket incident, but the others are new to me. Couldn't it just be normal teenage stunts that we all do in high school?

—Perhaps, but I see other things in his personality that concern me. When he's not causing noticeable disturbances, he's somewhat withdrawn. He's stopped combing his hair, he slumps in his seat, and he keeps his head down on the desk unless I constantly remind him to sit up and pay attention. Is he getting enough sleep at night?

—From what I observe, kids that age forget to comb their hair half the time anyway. And with all the new hair styles that the kids are coming up with, there's no telling what he's planning to do with his hair next week. And, as far as I know, he's getting plenty of sleep. He doesn't have an after-school job because of basketball. He's in his room most nights by eleven o'clock, and from what you say, he's not using a lot of his time to do homework, so that doesn't seem to be a problem. Besides, he never was a "morning person." He doesn't really get moving until noon.

—Well, I just wanted to let you know that I'm concerned. A couple of weeks ago, he ran out of the room in tears in the middle of a discussion about the suicide of Lady Macbeth. Let me ask you this—and please don't misunderstand my intentions or think that I'm trying to intrude into the personal life of your family—but wasn't Andy seeing a counselor about possible problems that may have been caused by his involvement in that accident?

—Yes, he was, initially. But the counselor has told me that he feels that Andy is adjusting quite well to the situation, and we will be discontinuing those sessions on a regular basis. I appreciate your efforts, but I feel that you might be overly concerned about a situation that is under control.

—I see. Well, thank you for your time. I hope Andy is able to get himself together and pass English this quarter. I'd hate to see him fail.

—I'll talk to him. You'll see an improvement. That's a promise.

LIONS, TIGERS, AND DINOSAURS

Andy and Monty at Home

FEBRUARY 20

—Hey, Monty, what's up? Watcha doin' there, little brother?

—Hi, Andy. I'm colorin' this picture for my teacher. It's real live homework, just like you do.

—Yeah, I wish mine was still that easy. Is that a poster for Brotherhood Week?

—Yep. It says, "All for one and one for all."

—Hey, that's pretty good reading for a little dude.

—This is nothin'. Last week, my teacher gave me a book with *chapters* in it. Watcha think of that?

—Chapters? I didn't know they put chapters in first-grade books. You too heavy for me. How come all the people in your picture got yellow hair?

—'Cause that's the prettiest color hair. These are special people in my picture and I want them to look real nice, so they gonna have yellow hair.

—You crazy, kid. What about this little girl here? She looks black to me—she's got fuzzy little braids and a real nice smile. Don't you have any brown crayons?

—Nope. She gonna have fuzzy little *yellow* braids.

—Why don't you make her look like Keisha? She's got pretty brown skin and curly black hair. You like Keisha, don't you?

—She's okay. You the one that's crazy about Keisha, not me. *I* like girls with yellow hair.

—You're a hopeless little dude, Monty.

—Actually, I like colorin' Africa pictures better than this kind of pictures—with no people in it. You know—lions and tigers and dinosaurs and stuff.

—Lions and tigers and *dinosaurs*?? That's some combination.

—Yep, and giraffes and dragons too. Hey, Andy, can I ask you somethin'?

—Sure, kid. Lay it on me.

—Do tigers cry?

—I don't know, Monty. I never thought about it, but I don't think they do. Why do you ask?

—Well, I drew a picture last week at school, and the teacher wanted to know why I put tears on my tiger. I told her he was very sad. Like you get sometime.

—You're somethin' else, little man. If you want to put tears on your tiger or dragons in your jungle, you tell your teacher that your big brother said it was just fine.

—Okay. Hey, Andy, can you take me to see that new dinosaur show at the museum?

—No, buddy, I can't—I can't drive—remember?

—Oh, did you forget how to drive?

—No, I'm not allowed to drive anymore.

—Why? Were you bad?

—Yes, Monty, I was bad. I was really, really bad. . . . Now go wash your hands and get ready for dinner.

HIDDEN OPINIONS

Conversation between Teachers

FEBRUARY 25

—How's that Andy Jackson doing in your class, Sheila?

—Well, he was no superstar to begin with. I guess now he's somewhere between failing miserably and squeaking by with mercy. He's not a bad kid. I understand he's pretty good in basketball. Maybe that will be his escape. That's what they all think anyway.

—Does he seem like he's bouncing back from that accident he was in a few months back? Wasn't he in counseling for a while?

—Yes, but I understand he's been dismissed by the psychiatrist as "stable."

—Stable? Look, I had Robbie Washington in my history class and it still upsets me. That kid watched his best friend die. How could he be stable after only three months?

—You know what? Just between the two of us, I don't think that accident affected him that much. Black kids are tough. They see a lot in life that we never experience. For example, that kid Gerald Nickelby, whose stepfather beats him up. Everybody knows about it. The police arrest his dad every few months or so. They go to court and Gerald ends up right back down there with the stepfather regaining custody. Like I said, they're tough. A white kid would have cracked under the pressure that Andy went through. But do you know what Andy does? He's always cracking jokes and making the other kids laugh. That young fool set off a bottle rocket from my window last month. The kids thought it was hilarious. They were all standing by the window cheering, when I walked in.

—Yes, you may be right. I heard he was going to be the master of ceremonies for that awful talent show they have. There's no real talent. All they have is that loud, disgusting rap music. Remember last year? That sweet little Donna Correlli was booed off the stage when she tried to sing opera.

—Oh, don't get me started about rap music . . . meaningless, mindless noise. Well, there's the bell. I'm giving my first bell a pop quiz. Don't forget the human relations committee meeting tonight after school.

—Okay, see you then.

NEEDS AND WORRIES

Keisha's Diary Entry

MARCH 9

March 9

Dear Diary,

Well, it's been five months today, since me and Andy started going together. October 9—March 9. It's been the roughest five months of my life, with the accident and everything. But Andy is so sweet, and so cute, and so—needing. It's like he really needs me to keep going. Sometimes it's nice, but I hate to say it, sometimes it gets on my nerves a little. Like last week, he was over here, and we were playing Ping-Pong in the basement, and he just goes and sits down on the couch and puts his head on his lap. I said, "Hey, Andy, watcha do—swallow the ball?" But he didn't smile—he looked up at me, and he had tears in his eyes, and he said, "Sometimes it just gets to me, you know?"

I get tired of all this depressing stuff. I miss Robbie too, but Andy can't seem to get over it, and I'm the only one who knows it. He's got his parents, his teachers, even that stupid counselor at the Outpatient Psych Center fooled. They all say stuff like, "Andy sure is adjusting well," because he's smiling and cheerful. He even volunteered to be the Master of Ceremonies at the Talent Show at school this month, and you ought to see him at practice, acting the fool up there on stage, rapping and dancing and grinning in the microphone. But I'm the one who has to listen to him when he calls me up just to ask, "What do you think it feels like to be dead?" or "Do you think Rob is cold tonight—it's so cold tonight" or "If I died, would you miss me?"

I'd like to ease up on our relationship a little, but I don't know how without hurting him. Well, he needs me, and he has been through a lot. I'm sure not going to be the one to cause him any more pain. But it sure does seem like Rhonda and Tyrone are having more fun.

"DO YOU? DO YOU?"

Rhonda's Letter to Tyrone (Passed to Him during Chemistry Class)

MARCH 15

Dear Tyrone,

Last night when you told me you loved me, did you really mean it? Because I <u>love</u> ice cream, and I <u>love</u> the Cincinnati Reds, and I even <u>love</u> my little sister. But the <u>real</u> kind of love scares me. I'm afraid that if I let myself love you, I might get hurt.

I know that I love being with you and I love the way you make me laugh. I love the way you're nice to my little sister and the way you're respectful and polite to my father. I love the way you offer to help my mother with the dishes. And I love the way you look at me across the room in chemistry class.

You make everything seem shiny and special. I've been to the zoo a million times, but when I went with you, it seemed exciting and fun. From counting mounds of elephant poop to watching the peacock spread his tail feathers—you made it wonderful. You have a way of making things that are ordinary seem really extraordinary. You make me feel like the most beautiful girl in the world. And you make me tingle when I'm near you. But I wasn't sure if what I was feeling was love or just happiness.

So last night, when you told me that you loved me, I could hardly catch my breath. I couldn't say anything at first because the whole idea was so overwhelming. I think I love you too, Tyrone, so please don't get mad at me if I ask you just once more. When you told me you loved me last night, did you really, really mean it?

Rhonda

"I DO"

Tyrone's Letter to Rhonda (Passed to Her during English Class)

MARCH 15

Dear Rhonda,

YES.

Tyrone

PUBLIC PLEASURE, PRIVATE PAIN

Talent Show at School

MARCH 30

—Ladies and Gentlemen!! Welcome to the Fifteenth Annual Hazelwood High School Talent Show. And I, Andrew Marvelous Jackson the First, will be your magnificent Master of Ceremonies! We'll be rappin' and scratchin' and bumpin' and jumpin'! We gonna electrify your senses and bombard your brain with the sounds that make you want to get down! So, *let's get busy!!!*

—Rhonda, come here. You wanna see a striptease show from backstage? Stand here by the curtain so they can't see you from the audience.
—Girl, Keisha, what are you talkin' about?
—Look at Andy! Look what he's doin'!

—He's takin' off his clothes! No, he's just pretendin'. Wait a minute—he took off his shirt! Everybody's dyin' laughin'! Oh, no! He wouldn't dare! He's unbucklin' his belt! This is *too* funny! Keisha, he's crazy!

—Rhonda, look! Mrs. Jawes is starting down the aisle! I don't think she finds it very funny.

—Psst, Andy! Old Thunder Jaws is headin' your way!

—Whew! He's putting his shirt back on. And the song is almost over. Did she go back to her roost?

—Yeah, but she's got daggers in her eyes.

—Rhonda, speaking of eyes, could you see Andy's face while he was dancing out there?

—The lights made it hard to see, but yeah, I did notice that his face looked funny.

—You know, with all that laughter and silliness out there, *Andy wasn't smiling.* Shhh, here he comes . . .

—You're doing a great job out there, Andy. They love you. That was *so* funny when you pretended to do that striptease in the background while Rashawn was singing, "Baby, Baby, Please!"

—Yeah, yeah, yeah. Is your group ready to sing, Keisha? If you'd spend more time gettin' yourself together and less time spyin' on me, this show could get over with by midnight. We ain't got all night, you know.

—Hey, you don't have to talk to me like that! I was just trying to compliment your stupid behind!

—What did I say? I just asked you if you were ready.

—It was the *way* you said it.

—Sometimes you get on my nerves, Keisha.

—Me? You've got to be kidding! Do you know what I put up with from you? If I hear one more sob story from you, I think I'll puke!

—So that's the way you feel about it! I thought you cared! I thought you were the only one in the world who really, really, cared!

—I *do* care, Andy. It's just that sometimes it's just too much!

—Why don't you just go to hell!

—I believe that's what I'm getting out of. Good-bye, Andy.

—Wait a minute! You can't leave! What about your song?

—*You* sing it!

PRIVATE PAIN

Andy and His
Mom at Home

MARCH 30
11:00 P.M.

—Andy, you're home early. How was the talent show?

—What do *you* care? You didn't bother to come.

—You know I've had a sinus headache, dear. Where's Keisha? I thought you two had planned to watch a movie on cable tonight.

—She went home. She had a headache. I guess it's something all women get.

—Well, fix yourself something to eat, and I'm going to turn in. I have a sorority meeting here tomorrow, so don't muss up the house.

—Yeah, whatever.

—Andy, is there anything wrong? You seem a little distracted tonight.

—No, Mom. I'm fine. I had a little fight with Keisha, that's all.

—I'm sure you two will work it out. She's such a nice young lady. I think she's been real good for you—helping you through the difficult times of the last few months.

—I'm surprised you noticed. You're right. She was probably the best thing that coulda happened to me. I didn't deserve her. That's why I lost her.

—No, don't talk like that. You deserve the very best that life has to offer. As time goes on, and we learn to put that "unfortunate incident" behind us, you'll find that your life will be full of wonderful opportunities, as well as lots of wonderful girls like Keisha.

—I wish you'd quit callin' it "the unfortunate incident"! It wasn't an "incident"! It was a crash! A terrible, terrible crash! And it was my fault! You need a dose of reality, Mom. You want to pretend it didn't happen and I can't deal with this by myself.

—You're right, Andy. The reality hurts. I guess my way of dealing with it is to hide from it.

—I've tried hidin', runnin', even dreamin'. Nothin' works. Hey, Mom, do you remember when I was nine, and we went on vacation to South Carolina?

—Sure. It was one of the nicest we ever went on.

—Yeah, if I remember, you even got in the water and let your hairdo get all messed up. I think that's probably the first, and last time, that I ever saw you without a "proper" hairdo.

—Well, I try to keep myself looking good.

—Oh, how well I know.

—So why did you bring up that vacation? Does it remind you of a time when things were better?

—Not really. Somethin' happened on that vacation that I never told you 'bout.

—What? What do you mean? What makes you bring it up now?

—'Cause the way I felt then is the way I feel tonight.

—I don't follow.

—Do you remember that boy in the next cabin? He was about twelve, and we played on the beach together every day.

—Vaguely. Yes, now that you mention it. I remember you playing with an older boy quite a bit.

—Well, on the night before we were to leave for home, he and I sneaked out to see if we could catch crabs on the beach in the moonlight. You and Dad were asleep.

—Keep going.

—Well, we couldn't find any crabs, so we decided to go wadin' in this little pool of water that had collected near some rocks on the beach.

—A tide pool?

—Yeah, I guess that's what it was. Anyway, it was a lot deeper than we thought it was, so we were goin' to go back before our parents noticed that we were gone, when I slipped.

—Oh my goodness! Then what happened?

—It was dark, so I couldn't see, and I was under the water, so I couldn't breathe. I tried to scream, but water got into my mouth and my throat and my chest. I was cryin' out for help, but my cries only made things worse. That's how I feel tonight, Mom. That's *exactly* how I feel tonight.

—So how did you get out of there? Why didn't you tell us?

—That kid pulled me out, dried me off, and hit me on the back until I stopped coughin' and started breathin' normally again. Then he made me promise never to tell what happened, or he would find me and beat me up. I was just glad to be out of there, so I crept back into bed, and never said a word. I figured the kid wouldn't have to beat me up—you'd kill me if you had found out. But you're missin' my point. I didn't bring this up to tell you about a dumb stunt I pulled when I was nine. I'm trying to explain how I feel tonight.

—Well, this is quite a revelation. You're right. I probably *would* have punished you. No doubt about it. And I want to help you now, Andy, but I don't know how. I just know that *time* heals all wounds, and that you're young and strong and resilient. You'll bounce back from this. Just like that time, when you were nine, you survived, and you emerged from that pool a stronger and wiser person. It will happen again. You'll see. My headache is getting worse. Let's talk some more in the morning. Good-night, Andy.

—Good-night, Mom. . . .

She doesn't understand that this time there's no one to pull me out. . . . I bet her headache is *nothin'* compared to mine. Maybe I should call that Carrothers dude. Naw, I can handle this. I don't need Keisha. She was wastin' my time anyway. If I could just shake off the fuzziness I feel. I can't sleep. I can't eat. I feel like the world is closin' in on me. I'm drowning again, only this time, Mom, I'm in an ocean. . . .

Naw, I can handle it. I can handle it.

"GIRL, LET ME TELL YOU!"

Rhonda's Second Letter to Saundra

APRIL 1

April 1

Dear Saundra,

Guess what! Andy and Keisha broke up the other night! Ooh, girl, you should have been there! It was at the Talent Show. Andy was Master of Ceremonies, and he was dealing! It was really live! The music was loud and the teachers were all lined up in the back of the auditorium, frowning, so you know it was good.

He seemed like he was having a good time. He's been really depressed lately—I guess because of the accident—but last night he was acting really silly. He had us cracking up! He did this striptease, where he took off his coat, and his shirt, and was about to unzip his pants. Mrs. Jawes was halfway down the aisle, but the song stopped. We was dying laughing.

Then, for some reason that I'm not really sure of, Andy and Keisha started fighting backstage. She was supposed to sing

141

that new song by Whitney Houston——I forget the name——
and dedicate it to Andy. It was going to be a surprise for him,
you know, to make him feel good about himself. She and I had
planned the whole thing.

But she never even went on. She stormed out of backstage
and went home. Then Andy came out on stage and announced,
almost in tears, that Keisha's act was canceled. I got to give
him credit——he did finish the show, but it was no fun after that.
All he did was read the names of each group and then go backstage and sit down.

I called Keisha as soon as I got home and asked her
what had happened. She told me that she was tired of holding his
hand and nursing him through his temper tantrums and crying
spells. She said she was glad it was over finally. She didn't have
the nerve to break up with him before this. I don't know what
Andy is going to do now. She told him they could still be
friends, but Andy needs more than that. I feel sorry for him,
but I side with Keisha——she ain't no shrink. That dude needs
help.

Me and Tyrone are still cool. I wish you could see the
dress I got for the Prom. He will just die! when he sees me.
Ooowee! That boy turns me on! Gotta run. I'll write again
when I can.

Love,
Rhonda

SLIPPING AWAY

Andy and the
Coach at School

APRIL 2

—Hey, Andy. I haven't seen you since basketball season ended. How've you been?

—Oh, just great, Coach Ripley. My grades are up. Me and Keisha are really tight. I got my act together; I'm even lookin' at colleges for next year.

—That's good to hear, Andy. I'm so glad you got over that bout of depression you had a couple of months back. That was a rough time for you. It will *always* be difficult to deal with, Andy, but taking one day at a time, with a positive attitude, is the only way to do it. Speaking of colleges, I do have a little bad news for you, however.

—What's that?

—Well, a couple of days ago some basketball scouts were here from Ohio State and Michigan State—friends of mine from college—and they were looking for you.

—Me?

—Yes, you. I had told them about you and how much you had improved this year, and how well you were scoring and rebounding, and they wanted to talk to you, maybe even shoot a few with you at my house, but you weren't at school that day.

—Uh, I had a cold. I stayed home a day or two.

—I called your house that evening too, trying to catch up with you, but all I got was your dad's answering machine. Did you get my message to call me?

—No, he never told me you called. Are the scouts comin' back?

—It's possible, I guess, if you have a real good finish to the year, but you really blew your chance to meet them informally and let them have the next few weeks to be thinking about scholarship possibilities for you.

—Well, uh, I know I'll get another chance. You wait and see. Scouts from all over will be here to check me out.

—I thought you'd be really upset, but you're really taking this well. I know how much you want to play college ball. It's good to see a smile on your face again.

—You're right, Coach. I got a smile on my

face and a bounce in my step. I'm gonna make it.

—Fantastic. Stop by my office any time you need to talk. See ya.

—College scouts? And I missed 'em? My dad makes me sick. It's all his fault. I'll never get a scholarship now. When they see my low grades, all my absences, and my police record, they'll break their necks runnin' away. . . . I don't care. I don't care. Who needs college anyway? I don't need college. I don't need basketball. I don't need Keisha. I don't need nothin'!

A FATHER'S DREAMS

Andy and His Dad at Home

APRIL 2
4:00 P.M.

—Hi, Dad, you're home early. What's to eat? I'm starved!

—Hello, Andrew. Is this the usual time you get home from school?

—Yeah, I guess—give or take a few. Why?

—Somehow I thought you got home after dark on most evenings.

—Well, I did, during basketball season, but that's been over for a couple of months now. So I just take the bus right after school and come on home.

—I see. How have you been doing in school? Are your grades any better?

—You want some of this ham sandwich? Sure is good. Where's the mustard?

—Andrew, I asked you a question.

—Huh? Oh, grades? No problem, Dad. I'm

steady pullin' 'em up. Is Monty home yet? The Teenage Warrior Space Soldier show is about to come on.

—Monty is with your mother. They went to the grocery store, I believe. But it's you I'm concerned about. Your report card came in today's mail.

—I'm dead meat.

—How can you possibly say your grades are improving? You failed English and chemistry, and you just barely passed history and math! You even failed gym! How can you consider yourself an athlete if you can't even pass gym?

—I lost my gym shoes.

—You what?

—I lost my shoes, and the gym teacher takes off points if you're not dressed in proper gym clothes. But I found 'em. They were in Gerald's locker.

—Forget gym. What about English and chemistry? I talked to your English teacher a couple of months ago, and it seemed for a while there that you were improving. What happened?

—I don't know. She don't like me.

—That's a weak excuse, Andrew. She seemed genuinely concerned when she called me. That doesn't sound like someone who doesn't like you. Have you done all your assignments in her class?

—Yeah, most of 'em. . . . Well, some of 'em.

—What about tests?

—What about 'em?

—Don't play with me, boy. I'm trying to figure out what's going on here. How do you usually do on her tests?

—I guess I fail most of 'em.

—Do you study for the tests?

—Sometimes.

—How can you say you want to go to college? What college is going to take you with grades like this?

—I never said I wanted to go to college. *You* were the one who said I wanted to go to college.

—What do you mean? We've been talking about college since you were a little boy! Getting a degree—maybe even in the field of business administration.

—That's your dream, Dad, not mine.

—Well, what about basketball? Didn't you want to go to college to play ball so you could get a chance at professional basketball? You've really improved your game this year.

—How would you know? You didn't ever come to even one of my games this year! Not one!

—Well, you know how hectic my schedule is. Besides, I've seen you in the yard when you shoot hoops with your friends. I know you're good.

—Yeah, right.

—But back to the subject at hand—this absolutely reprehensible report card!

—Why you gotta always use such big words? I know my report card stinks. Why can't you just say that?

—If you had a better vocabulary, perhaps you wouldn't be failing English!

—Why don't you just get off my case?

—I'm not going to argue with you, Andrew. But I expect to see some major improvements in these last couple of months of school. Or I shall have to take some severe punitive measures.

—There you go with them big words again. What else can you do to punish me? Take away my car? It's in pieces at Joe's Auto Graveyard. Take away my driver's license? Sorry, the cops beat you to that. Stop me from seein' my best friend? He's in pieces at Spring Grove People Graveyard. I took care of that myself—I killed him—remember? So, you can't hurt me. I deal with big-time hurt every day.

—Andrew, I know the accident was very traumatic for you. But you have to get beyond it and move on. You have to be strong and show that you are bigger than the problem.

—Yeah, I know. You've told me that before. Be a man. Be strong. Put this "unfortunate incident" behind you. Well, maybe I can't do that.

—So you're going to let it control your actions and ruin your life?

—No, Dad. I'm gonna get it together. You'll see. My grades for the last quarter of school will be much better—I promise.

—That's my Andrew. I know you can do it, son. I'm counting on you. Don't let me down now, okay? Do it for me.

—Okay, Dad. Whatever you say. . . . Hey, Dad. . . . Can I ask you a question?

—Sure, Andrew.

—How come you always call me "Andrew"? Mom, Monty, all my friends, even my teachers—they all call me "Andy." But you never have. And I've never had the nerve to ask you why.

—Well, son, let me tell you. My father named me Ezekiel Jeremiah Jackson—two strong Bible names—he had great ambitions for me. But that name turned out to be a detriment rather than an asset to me. When I was growing up, kids called me "Zeke" and even "Eazy," and I hated it.

—Hah! Eazy Jackson. I love it!

—Well, I hated it. I wanted so much to be dignified and respectable and proper.

—Well, you sure got that!

—Quit interrupting. I'm trying to explain where I'm coming from. You see, I wanted to be—

—White?

—No, not white, but accepted by them. And it was almost impossible to be taken seriously in the business world with a name like "Ezekiel." I'd be sitting in a meeting with a group of five or six of them, all of us in blue suits and serious ties. The meeting would go something like this:

"Bob, what do you think the strategy should be?"

"Well, Tom, let's get a market sample."

"Bill, did you get the printouts of the data?"

"Yes, and Ezekiel here did the sales analysis."

—Then there'd be this silence while they tried not to giggle. It just didn't work. And "Zeke" was worse. They all had a black handyman at home named "Zeke." So I started calling myself "E. J." They seemed to respect and accept that. Besides, all the presidents of all the big companies refer to themselves as "T. W." or "J. B." They were used to the format, at least. So that's why I'm known at work simply as E. J. Jackson. I don't think there's anyone there who knows my real name, except maybe the people in personnel.

—Is that why you're always so nice to B. J.?

—Maybe. He seems like a nice fella, though. What's his real name?

—He said his mama won't even tell him, and he don't wanna know!

—Well, I can understand where he's coming from.

—I wish you could understand where *I'm* comin' from sometimes.

—What was that you said? You were mumbling.

—Nothin'. Thanks for tellin' me that. I mean, I knew your name and all that, but you never told me why you never used it. But you still haven't explained why you always call me Andrew.

—When you were born, I wanted to give you something my father had tried, but failed, to give me—a name to be proud of. I didn't want you to have to shorten it or lighten it in any way. So, from the time you were little, I called you Andrew. I guess it was partly from pride, and partly from this determination that I had to make you something really special.

—I ain't nothin' special.

—Well, your grades don't show it, but you *are*! You should be in the top of your class, showing everybody, both black and white, that E. J. Jackson's son is somebody to be respected and admired.

—How come I gotta be E. J. Jackson's

son? How come I can't be just plain old ordinary Andy Jackson?

—Because ordinary isn't good enough!

—Why not?

—Look, I went to college—night school for six years—while I worked at various jobs during the day to make ends meet. I studied all the time. I carried a dictionary with me wherever I went so that I could improve my vocabulary. I was always conscious of improving myself—making myself better—making myself good enough, bright enough, proper enough, respectable enough.

—For what?

—For my co-workers. For myself.

—You think they care that you busted your butt to be acceptable to them?

—It's that desire to excel that I see lacking in you. Sometimes I think you just don't care.

—Sometimes you're right.

—How can you *not* care about your life, Andr . . . Andy?

—You seem to be doin' a fine job of dreamin' my dreams and plannin' my future. Maybe I don't wanna be acceptable to white folks.

—But you *must*! That's the only way to make it in this world—to assimilate into the society in which we live. *That's* why you must pull up your grades and improve your attitude. That is the key to success.

—What if I can't?

—I'm not taking "no" for an answer. You *will* show substantial improvement. I will not accept anything less than maximum effort. *No son of mine is going to be a failure!* Do you hear me?

—Okay, Dad. Whatever you say.

—There's your mother's car in the driveway. Help her bring in the groceries.

—I hope she didn't get much. I'm not very hungry anymore.

NIGHTTIME CRIES OF DESPERATION

Andy's Final Phone Calls

APRIL 2
MIDNIGHT

—Maybe I should call Keisha. Naw, I've had enough of her whinin' and complainin'. And I thought she understood me! She ain't nothin' but a scar on my soul. I gotta move on.

—I think I'll call that Carrothers dude. He said to call him anytime—day or night. Let's see—what's that number? Here it is. Maybe if I talk to him, I can get my head clear. I feel like I got cotton in my brain.

—Hello, this is Dr. Carrothers's answering service. May I help you?

—Uh, yeah. My name is Andy Jackson, and I need to talk to Dr. Carrothers—right away.

—Are you a patient of his?

—Yeah, I guess. I've been in to see him several times. He said it was okay for me to call him anytime of the day or night. So I'm callin'. Could you connect me, please?

—I'm sorry, sir, but Dr. Carrothers's mother had a heart attack and he had to go out of town. Dr. Kelly is taking his calls tonight. He'd be very glad to talk to you.

—Dr. Kelly? Who is that? I can't talk to no stranger. It took me a long time to get used to talkin' to that one long-head doctor. And he told me he'd be there for me anytime I needed him. This is the first time I feel like I really need to talk to him, and you tell me he ain't there? What kinda mess is this?

—Sir, Dr. Carrothers *was* the doctor on call tonight, but as I told you, he had a sudden emergency. I can get Dr. Kelly to—

—Look, isn't there some way you can call Dr. Carrothers long-distance? This is really important.

—I'm really sorry, . . . you said your name was Andy?

—Yeah, Andy.

—I'm really very sorry, Andy. Dr. Carrothers left about two hours ago for the airport, headed for California. He's on the plane now, so we can't even page him. But Dr. Kelly is a really fine adviser, and I know you'll like him. Let me connect you—he's on the other line. He'll be with you in thirty seconds, okay?

—Yeah, okay . . . *click* . . . Forget this! I don't need this. How come he be gone? Adults are always talkin' 'bout bein' there when you need them, but then when you decide you do, they be disappeared like dust!

—Okay. What do I do now? I feel like the world is closin' in on me. Wait a minute! I know who's home. Coach Ripley. Of course he's home. Tomorrow is a school day. He's gotta go to work. He's gotta be home. He'll cheer me up. He always makes sense. I wonder if he's asleep.

—Hello, you have reached the Ripley residence. We're sorry we are unable to come to the phone now. If you leave a message at the sound of the tone, we'll get back to you as soon as possible. Have a real nice day. . . . BEEP!

—. . . *Click*. . . .

—Yeah, well *you* have a real nice day, or night, or life, or whatever! I *hate* talkin' to machines. It's like it takes a part of you, a part of your soul or something, when you talk on those things. You leave a little piece of yourself, all naked and unprotected, for anybody to see when they push the little button. Well, they ain't gettin' none of me. Coach is probably asleep anyway. I'll talk to him tomorrow at school.

—School. . . . When I think about school, I feel like I got a mouth full of dry bread and I can't swallow. . . . When I think about school, I feel like I jumped off the deep end of the pool, then remembered that I couldn't swim, and then realized that it didn't matter anyway because the pool was empty. . . . When I think about school, I feel like I'm tryin' to take deep breaths, but the air is made of sand. . . . When I think about school, I feel like I'm in a dark, closed room, with invisible hands pushin' me from all directions, pushin' me toward a light I can't see. Some kids can see the light. Some walk around like they got lights screwed in their foreheads. Some just carry a glow, like Keisha. Yeah, Keisha shines. I'm gonna call her. She'll talk to me. I know she will.

—Hello, Mrs. Montgomery? May I speak to Keisha, please.

—Who is this?

—It's me, Andy Jackson. Did I wake you up?

—Andy? Of course you woke me up. Do you know what time it is?

—I'm sorry. I really need to speak to Keisha. It's important.

—Andy, she's asleep, and you should be too. You can't call here after midnight on a school night and expect me to call her to the phone. I don't care how important it is. Now you go get some rest and you can talk to her at school tomorrow, okay?

—I'm sorry I bothered you, Mrs. Montgomery. Don't even tell her I called. She'll just have one more thing to be mad at me for.

—Things always look brighter in the

morning, Andy. I'm sure you two will be able to work out your differences. She really thinks a lot of you. Now get off this phone and let me get back to sleep!

—Okay, Mrs. M. Good night, and thanks.

—So what do I do now? My head is throbbin'. My mind is cloudy. My heart is bloody, and my soul is on ice. (I think I read that somewhere. . . .) Nobody's home. Nobody cares. Maybe I'll try to sleep. I wish I could sleep forever.

"HAVE YOU
SEEN ANDY?"

Andy's Friends
at School

APRIL 3

IN HOMEROOM

—Grimes?

—Here.

—Hawkins?

—Yeah.

—Henderson?

—Here.

—Immerman?

—Over here.

—Jackson? . . . Jackson? . . . Is Andy
absent again?

—Yeah, Mr. Whitfield. He's got "senioritis,"
a terrible disease.

—I'd say that he might have a fatal disease. Students who catch "senioritis" have
been known to develop serious compli-

cations and never graduate.

—He'll be here tomorrow. He has to. He owes me two dollars.

—Good luck. Okay, let's finish with attendance.

—Johnson?

—Here . . .

—Keisha, have you seen Andy?

—No, and I hope I never do again.

—Come on, girl, you know it hurts.

—Yeah, Rhonda. It hurts. I really liked him, you know, but it just got too complicated. He's better off without me. He's got to get himself together before he can get seriously involved with someone else. How's Tyrone?

—Oh, just great. We're goin' to the movies tomorrow. Do you want to come?

—No. I'll probably just catch a movie on cable. It's kinda nice just to relax for a change and not worry about how I look or what I'll wear or where we're going. I'm just going to chill and enjoy my freedom.

—Okay, but call me if you change your mind. Say, I'm going to drop off Andy's chemistry homework to his house after school. Mr. Whitfield said he'd fail unless he got this assignment in. You wouldn't want to go with me, would you?

—No way, girl. Actually, if I saw him, I

might break down and do something stupid like cry, or make up with him. I'm out of his life—at least for now.

—Okay. I'll call you later.

TIGERS HAVE IT ROUGH

Andy—at Home Alone

APRIL 3
10:00 A.M.

—So what do I do now? Pray? Cry? Hide under the bed from the monsters that are inside of me? No, I'm just going to sit here and think. I'm goin' to think about why I'm sittin' here on my bed, holdin' my dad's huntin' rifle, feelin' how smooth and cool it feels. He likes to hunt— some killer instinct left over from his ancestors who ran around in loincloths in the Congo. Ha! What would they think if they could see him in his three-piece suit, spear in hand, crouchin' low to stalk a tiger?

Tigers have it rough these days. Instead of roamin' the jungle, hiding from hunters in three-piece loincloths, they are put in concrete cages with bars of steel. Even in the modern zoos, where it looks like the tigers ought to be happy because they are given fifteen or twenty feet of real grass, if you look really hard, you can see tiny little electrical wires. The tiger, who might think he's equal to all those tigers in the jungle that his mama told him about, is quickly reminded to stay in his place. He soon learns that he'll never get out of there.

I've always hated this bedspread. It's lumpy and when you sit on it, little tufts of the material stick to your clothes. See, it's already started— tiny little bits of lint all over my slacks. And it always slides off my bed in the middle of the night, just when I'm sleeping too hard to know it's gone. I just have this vague feelin' I'm cold, or dreamin' of being cold, or somethin'.

I'm a little cold now—now that I think about it—cold inside, like there's nothin' there, or like my guts are frozen. I remember once when I was little I got this same frozen-gut feelin'. I was in a department store with Mama and we were on the escalator—goin' down. I remember feelin' slightly dizzy as I looked behind us at where we'd been, the steps rollin' smoothly. When we got to the bottom, the shoe-string of my new red tennis shoes got caught and the steps kept rollin', pullin' me and my foot with them. Mama screamed, and I guess I was scared, because I just felt frozen—like I was watchin' myself on TV—as the movin' steps gradually gobbled my shoestring and pulled my foot toward its teeth. Some dude ran over to the escalator and pushed the emergency button. Mama pulled me loose, and then smacked me for being careless. I never even cried. I just felt like I wasn't really there—like now, sittin' here on my bed, wishin' that I was nowhere at all.

It's not that I want to die—it's just that I can't stand the pain of livin' anymore. I just want the hurt and pain inside to go away. It's like a monster in my gut—eatin' me up from the inside out. Actually, I feel like the only thing that's keepin' me from going crazy is this terrible, terrible pain.

There's nobody home—everybody's gone for the day. I left for school, but halfway there I forgot where I was going, or why. So I came back here, to sit on my lumpy, linty bedspread, wishin' I had never been born, strokin' the smooth, cool barrel of my father's shotgun. It is very, very quiet.

I'm sorry for all I've done—so sorry, . . . so very, very sor—

FACTS WITHOUT FEELINGS

Official Police Report

APRIL 3
8:30 P.M.

OFFICIAL POLICE REPORT
YOUTH INVESTIGATIVE DIVISION

DATE: April 3

TIME: 1820

INVESTIGATING OFFICER: Casey

SUBJECT: Andrew Jackson—male—black, age 17

ADDRESS: 2929 Ridgemont Lane

FINDING: Suicide

DISPOSITION: Deceased

SUMMARY REPORT:

On the morning of April 3, the above-named student left for school, but a neighbor reported seeing him return home about one hour later. He never reported to school. His friends had expressed concern because of Andrew's recent extreme fits of depression. A friend, Rhonda Jeffries, arrived at the house at 4:05 to bring Andrew some missed schoolwork. Andrew's mother, who was just getting home from picking up her younger son from school, had not been aware that her son had not gone to school. The younger child, Monty, age six, noticed blood on the ceiling. Mrs. Jackson went to her son's bedroom where Andrew's body was found with a fatal gunshot wound to the head. Police and life squad were summoned at 4:11. Andrew was pronounced dead at the scene.

FEELINGS ON DISPLAY

Grief Counselor at School

APRIL 4
9:00 A.M.

—Good morning, class. My name is Mrs. Sweet and I'm a member of the suicide prevention/grief counseling team that has been brought in to help you through this crisis. We want you to feel free to express your emotions—so cry if you want to, or ask us questions—whatever you need to do to get through this.

—If you work for the suicide prevention team, you didn't do a very good job, did you?

—You sound bitter, young man. Your name is? . . .

—Tyrone. Andy was my friend. Where was you last month when me and B. J. was lookin' for somebody to help him? You got posters and emergency phone numbers for suicide prevention hot lines posted all over the building today. Where was you last week? What good does it do now?

—You have a point, Tyrone. Your counselors here at school know these numbers and should have had them available for you.

—When we went to see the counselor, all we got was bad breath and bad advice.

—There is no way that your counselor could have seen the future. I'm sure she would have suggested our number had she known the severity of Andy's problems.

—Yeah, sure. Tell me anythin'.

—Is there anyone else who would like to express their feelings? Anger is a perfectly normal emotion.

—Yes? Your name?

—B. J.

—B. J.? . . . uh . . . that stands for? . . .

—It stands for B. J. Mrs. Sweet, we've had two kids die in our class this school year. We had some people here from your office when Robbie died too. It didn't do no good then neither. They're still dead. And I'm afraid I'll be next. I'm just plain scared.

—As we get older, we all learn that death is a part of life. If we let these tragedies become growth experiences, if we learn from them, then we have in some way triumphed over the fear and anger and sorrow that death brings.

—That sounds like somethin' you got outta a book. That don't cover how I feel. Andy left without sayin' good-bye and I don't know why. He had friends that cared about him that he didn't ask for help. I feel like he punched me in the gut and I can't hit back.

—I understand. Does anyone else have anything to say? No one? I see. Sometimes it's hard to speak such personal emotions out loud. I have an idea. Suppose you could write a letter to Andy. Don't tell *me* what's on your mind, talk to *him*. Tell him what you wanted to say, what you wish you had said, what you want to say now. If you write it down, that might help you sort out your feelings.

—This is stupid.

—If you don't want to participate in this activity, that's perfectly acceptable. But for those of you who do, let's see if it helps.

ANGER AND PAIN

Letters to Andy
from His Friends

APRIL 8–12

Dear Andy,

Well, this stupid counselor woman said to write this
dumb letter to you. J don't see what for. Jt's supposed to
make us feel better. But how can we feel better if we still
don't understand <u>why</u>? Hey, man, life ain't perfect, but it's
<u>life</u>! Remember right after the accident when we realized
we wasn't going to die? Jn spite of all that noise and fire
and death, we looked at each other, and real quicklike,
we <u>smiled</u>. You know why? Cause we were <u>alive</u>. And
we were glad. Of course we felt horrible because Rob
was dead. J will never, never forget him, or that terrible
night. And we felt guilty too—guilty that it was our stupid
behavior that caused it, and guilty that we had lived and
he had died. J been able to deal with the guilt—day by
day it gets easier to handle. But <u>you</u>—you never got out
from under the blame you put on yourself.

We didn't die in that accident for a reason. B. J. says it's because the Lord needed Robbie up there and he needed us down here. (I guess you know B. J.'s gotten real religious lately.) I don't know about all that—all I know is that if there <u>was</u> some special reason why we didn't die in that crash, then you just blew it.

Robbie's death was an <u>accident</u>. Somehow I can deal with that, but what <u>you</u> did—it just don't make no sense to me. You're making everything so rough for the rest of us. Rhonda and Keisha—they cry every time you look at them; and me and B. J. try to hang together, but nothing is fun anymore. I probably never will figure all this out. I know my life will never be the same. But I also know that dying don't fix nothing. It just makes things worse. I don't know what I'm here for, but I'm here to stay, and I got the guts to keep on living and find out why.

I'll miss you, Andy, and I'll never forget you, but when me and Rhonda is married and got six kids, you won't be there. And when B. J. is preaching to a church with 5,000 people, you won't be there. And when Keisha is a famous fashion designer with a Ph.D. in chemistry, with all kinds of fine-looking dudes around her, you <u>still</u> won't be there.

So later, brother. Say hello to Romeo and Juliet for me. Tell them I think they were stupid too. They didn't get to go to the Senior Prom either.

Your main man,
Tyrone

Dear Andy,

You know what really pisses me off? <u>You!</u>
You're a coward and a sellout! You decided to
end your life, without saying good-bye to anybody, without asking anyone for help. You
deserted your friends and family—the people
who love you the most. Suicide is the coward's
way out. Brave men face their problems. So
what does that make you? I don't want to face
my problems either. So what does that make
me?

Do you know what courage is? I guess you
don't. Do you know that the courage it took at
that moment—to actually blow yourself away—
was more than enough courage to keep on living?
It takes courage for me to get out of bed every
morning, to put up with my stepfather's beatings,
with my house that stinks of pee, with my face
that looks at me in the mirror each morning and
reminds me that the scar is still there. But I
smile back at my face and I grab a bag of
potato chips and my basketball and I head out
for school. Because I have courage. I'll be here
next week. Where will you be?

I hate you for leaving me here. I hate you
for making me feel like this. I hate you for
making me cry. And I hate you for making me
face death again so soon.

Gerald

Dear Andrew,

   You don't know me very well. You probably don't know me at all. I was in your English class this year. I sat on the other side of the room, near the door. I'm the one with the torn book bag and the nondesigner jeans. I used to sit there and watch you—cracking jokes with the teacher, charming the girls with that freaky smile, and laughing when you flunked one of those pop quizzes. And I envied you. Oh yes, I envied your easy, careless ways. Sure, I got good grades. (You once stood up and led the whole class in a cheer for me because I was the only one who got a perfect score on the <u>Macbeth</u> test—I know you don't remember that—I'm one of those kids who's easily forgotten—but I'<u>ll</u> never forget it.) I wanted to be like you—popular and likable and well known. I never realized the price you were paying for that mask you were wearing. I'm glad I found out—I like myself a lot better now.

                                          Marcus

Dear Andy,

   I have some questions for you. Everyone has been asking why—why did you do it? Why now? Why didn't you ask for help? But I've got some harder questions for you.

   What were you thinking while sitting in your bedroom with that shotgun? Who did you think would find you? Did you have someone particular in mind? Your dad? Your mom? How about your little brother, Monty? He's six years old. Did you think what an effect this would have on the rest of his life? Did you think about the blood?——on your bed, the wall, the floor? Did you know the blood dripped through the floorboards through the ceiling of the living room? That's how they first discovered what you had done. Monty asked your mom why there was blood on the ceiling.

I'm not through with you. Your mom found you, or what was left of you. Did you think about her? Could you feel her pain as she walked into your room, and saw your body draped across your bed, a gun still clutched in your hand, and shattered segments of your head spread across a room which looked as if it had been painted with blood? Do you know what blood <u>smells</u> like, Andy? Your mom does. She'll never forget it. Part of her died that day too.

And so did I. I was there. I had come to bring your chemistry homework because you weren't at school. When she screamed, I ran upstairs. From that point, it's like a terrible videotape that keeps rewinding, that won't erase. The blood, the screams, the tears, the frantic call to 911, the ambulance, the police, the body bag. Then the numbness, more tears, the disbelief, and the questions. Then more tears, the wake, the funeral, and the pain——the pain that will not go away.

So, tell me. <u>What</u> were you thinking?

Rhonda

Dear Andy,

You can't be dead. But I went to your funeral. I felt your coffin. It was warm and woody, but you couldn't have been in it. I wanted to open it, to knock and call out your name, but I didn't dare. I went to the cemetery. I kept thinking, Everybody here is dead . . . they're all dead! Thousands and thousands of dead people——people who would never come back. And then I really did call out your name, and I finally cried. I wept for you—because you weren't supposed to be with all these dead people, because you can't, you just can't be dead.

So, I guess the pain is over for you now. You have moved to the place where there is no pain, and I guess that's good. But the pain left by your absence is like a wound in our hearts that will not heal. Nobody understands why you decided to end your life when you had so much to live for. So you're out of it and we have to stay here, feeling your pain as well as our own. It really isn't fair, you know.

Some people say (and don't get me wrong—you know how often I go to church), well, they say that killing yourself is a sin and you'll go to hell for it because you took a life that had been given by God, and you can never ask for forgiveness for that. But I can't _bear_ that thought, so in your case I hope God is forgiving. I hope God understands that your heart was good, but your pain was so powerful. (Of course, with that smart mouth of yours, God may be sorry and kick you out!)

I love you. Take care. Wait for me. . . .

Love,
Keisha

"LORD, PLEASE FORGIVE HIM."

B. J.'s Prayer for Andy

—Dear Lord, there's a dude named Andy who's on his way up there, at least I hope he's headed in Your direction. He's not a bad kid—just young and very, very stupid. Will stupidity keep him out of Heaven?

He suffered a lot down here. He never could talk to his folks and he stayed tied up in knots. He felt so very guilty for Robbie's death. I think it's because he never learned to pray. He never learned the power and hope that comes from Your forgiveness. I know that's what kept me sane.

He never willingly hurt anybody or anything. I remember once when we were in the eighth grade, Andy had a puppy who got hit by a car. He had only had the dog for a couple of weeks, so he couldn't have been that attached to it, but when it died, Andy almost fell apart. He stayed depressed for weeks.

I think Andy was scared of death in general. Two years ago, when old Mr. Mancilli, one of our gym teachers, died of a heart attack, a lot of the kids from school went to the funeral. But not Andy. He got all nervous and irritable whenever anybody even mentioned Mr. Mancilli. He just couldn't cope. The whole idea of death terrified him.

So I know Andy was afraid. His soul is probably still out there somewhere—floating in the darkness, looking for hope, hoping for forgiveness, and terribly, terribly frightened.

I know You already know all of this, but I just wanted to ask if You'd look out for my partner, and help him find peace.

THE TEARS OF A TIGER

Monty's Good-bye to Andy

MAY 15

—Andy? Can you hear me? It's me, Monty. Mama brought me here to the cemetery because I told her I just had to talk to you. She didn't want to come. She hasn't been back here since the funeral, but I kept buggin' her. She won't even get out of the car. She's over there now, just sittin' and cryin'. That's all she does now—cry. It's startin' to get on my nerves.

Things have changed a lot since you . . . since you . . . left. We live in another house now. Actually Mama and me live in one place, and Daddy lives somewhere else. I get to see him on weekends, but it's not the same. Nothin' is the same. The only good part is that they pay a whole lot of attention to me now. I got a computer for my birthday last week. You forgot I had *a birthday coming, didn't you? You forgot about me completely, didn't you?*

I miss you, Andy. Who's gonna teach me how to dribble down the court and make layups? How am I ever gonna learn to make free throws? You know how rotten Daddy is at basketball. His belly keeps gettin' in the way. And how am I ever gonna figure out girls? Do you know some girl tried to kiss me for my birthday? Gross!

It's a real pretty day today. It's warm and the sun is shinin' and everythin' smells real good. I wish you could see it. I wish you were here. I wish everything was like it used to be. Daddy says I gotta be brave and strong. I guess I can do that, but at night I get real scared and sometimes I have bad dreams. But I'm not going to cry anymore, 'cause I'm tough, like a tiger, and tigers don't cry, or do they?

Mama is callin' me now. She says it's time to go. I'm sure she wants me to tell you she's thinkin' about you always. I feel better now. I'm glad she let me come and talk to you. I don't know when I'll get to come again—I'm gonna start Knothole Baseball next week and I spend a lot of time learnin' how to use my computer, so you know how it is. But I'll always love you, and I'll always miss you, and I'll never forget that it's okay to put dragons in the jungle and tears on a tiger.

Bye.

A Reader's Guide to *Tears of a Tiger*

1. *Tears of a Tiger* begins with a tragic accident—a fatal car crash caused by drinking and driving. The story is then told from the points of view of the group of friends involved.

• How does this method of telling the story affect the reader's response?

• What advantages and disadvantages does this method of narrative offer?

2. Many teenagers drink and then drive without thinking about the consequences.

• How is Andy like many young people today?

• How is he different?

• What makes this book more than just a moral warning to readers about drinking and driving?

3. Describe the relationship between the friends in the book.

• How does Rob's death affect each of the young people, and how does it affect their relationships with each other?

• Is friendship enough when situations become monumental and overwhelming to young people?

4. What do you know of Hazelwood High School from the descriptions given in the text?

• How would you describe the building itself, the teachers, the students, the administration, the "feel" of the school?

• How does it compare to high schools in your community?

• Why is a high school a good place to discuss serious issues?

5. Basketball is a source of physical release for Andy, but it also raises strong feelings of guilt. He loves the game, but feels guilty that he is given Rob's position on the team—a position that Andy was never good enough for when Rob was alive.

• How are sports important in the lives of young people?

• What positive as well as negative results can sports play in the life of a teenager?

6. Andy's family had many problems. Andy's parents loved him, but seemed preoccupied with their own lives and were

helpless to see his pain. Andy could talk to his younger brother, Monty, but the six-year-old was unable to help with Andy's problems.

• How can families learn to cope effectively with tragedy and difficulties?

• How could Andy's family have dealt more successfully with Andy's situation?

7. Andy's parents send him to see a psychologist to help him "talk through" his problems—to deal with the guilt and trauma caused by Rob's death.

• How successful are the efforts of the psychologist, and how was Andy able to convince the psychologist that he was effectively dealing with his problems?

• What serious psychological issues are raised through Andy's conversations with Dr. Carrothers?

8. Describe Andy's gradual decline. Discuss all of the factors that contributed to Andy's suicide.

• Could Andy's death have been prevented? How?

• What are the reactions of Andy's friends to his death, and how do those reactions demonstrate that life is always a better solution than death?

9. What are the problems created by discussing the issue of teen suicide and death in a novel for young adults?

• What dangers and what positive influences can result?

• What is the effect of Monty's final words to Andy in the last chapter?

10. What do the poems and essays written by the various students reflect about their lives and personalities?

• Why are the poems and essays an easy way to explain complicated feelings?

• How can self-expression be used as a tool for helping or healing?

11. The teenagers in the novel are honest, realistic, and able to express themselves comfortably to each other and to the adults around them.

• Do teenagers speak two "languages"—one for themselves and one for adults?

• What is the effect of the use of modified slang in the conversations of the young people in the story?

• What is the effect of the conversational style of narration, which eliminates the use of traditional quotation marks as they speak to each other?

12. Explain the title of the novel. What references can be found to "tears" and to "tigers"?

• Why does the title have more than one possible interpretation?

13. Many people have asked the author why Andy was allowed to die at the end of the novel.

• What would have been the effect on the novel if Andy had lived?

• Why is tragedy more memorable and more powerful than happiness in a novel?

14. Imagine Monty in ten years, when he will be the age that Andy was when he died.

• How will Monty's life be different? The same?

• How will Monty's parents' attitudes toward him change?

• Will their family have been strengthened or completely destroyed by Andy's death?

15. Visualize the next ten years for Keisha, Gerald, and B. J.

• How will their lives be affected by the events of that year in high school?

• Create a scene in which they meet at a ten-year reunion. What will have happened to them and why?

ACTIVITIES AND RESEARCH

1. You are a reporter at one of the following scenes. Write the story for your newspaper.

—Andy's trial for the accident that caused Rob's death
—Rob's funeral
—Andy's funeral
—the session with the grief counselor at school

2. Investigate the organization called S.A.D.D. (Students Against Driving Drunk).

• What has been its effect in high schools?

• How have students been using positive peer pressure to stop the problem of teenage drinking and driving?

3. Investigate the recent laws concerning drivers under the age of eighteen who are involved in traffic fatalities.

• What is the usual punishment?

• Is Andy's punishment realistic or no longer true in many states?

• What do you think should be the punishment for young drivers who drink and cause the death of another person?

4. Investigate the problem of teenage suicide.

• What steps can be taken by schools to prevent this problem?

• How can friends help other friends who seem to be depressed or suicidal?

5. Write a letter to one of the characters in the book explaining your feelings about the events in the story.

• What advice would you give Keisha, Monty, or Andy's parents?

• What would you say to Andy?

6. Consider a career as a psychologist. Find out how much college education is needed, how many years of study it takes, and what is required to become a doctor of psychology as Dr. Carrothers was in the story.

• What other fields might offer counseling to young people?

• What are the requirements for those fields?

7. Create a scene in which the following two characters meet. What would they say to each other?

—Keisha and Andy just before Andy's death

—Andy and Rob's mother at the hospital

—Andy's coach and Andy's dad

—Andy and Rob after their deaths

8. Pretend you are a student at Hazelwood High School. Write a poem, a letter, or a journal entry on one of the following topics:

—Death at an early age

—It's tough to be a teen

—Forever friends

What's new from Sharon M. Draper?
Here is an excerpt from her stunning
new novel, *Copper Sun*.

IN SPITE OF THE HEAT, AMARI
TREMBLED. *The buyers of slaves had
arrived. She and the other women were
stripped naked. Amari bit her lip, determined
not to cry. But she couldn't stop herself from
screaming out as her arms were wrenched
behind her back and tied. A searing pain shot
up through her shoulders. A white man
clamped shackles on her ankles, rubbing his
hands up her legs as he did. Amari tensed and
tried to jerk away, but the chains were too
tight. She could not hold back the tears. It was
the summer of her fifteenth year, and this day
she wanted to die.*

*Amari shuffled in the dirt as she was led
into the yard and up onto a raised wooden
table, which she realized gave the people in
the yard a perfect view of the women who
were to be sold. She looked at the faces in the
sea of pink-skinned people who stood around
pointing at the captives and jabbering in their
language as each of the slaves was described.*

She looked for pity or even understanding but found nothing except cool stares. They looked at her as if she were a cow for sale. She saw a few white women fanning themselves and whispering in the ears of well-dressed men— their husbands, she supposed. Most of the people in the crowd were men; however, she did see a poorly dressed white girl about her own age standing near a wagon. The girl had a sullen look on her face, and she seemed to be the only person not interested in what was going on at the slave sale.

Amari looked up at a seabird flying above and remembered her little brother. I wish he could have flown that night, *Amari thought sadly.* I wish I could have flown away as well.

"WHAT ARE YOU DOING UP THERE, KWASI?" Amari asked her eight-year-old brother with a laugh. He had his legs wrapped around the trunk of the top of a coconut tree.

"For once I want to look a giraffe in the eye!" he shouted. "I wish to ask her what she has seen in her travels."

"What kind of warrior speaks to giraffes?" Amari teased. She loved listening to her brother's tales—everything was an adventure to him.

"A wise one," he replied mysteriously, "one who can see who is coming down the path to our village."

"Well, you look like a little monkey. Since you're up there, grab a coconut for Mother, but come down before you hurt yourself."

Kwasi scrambled down and tossed the coconut at his sister. "You should thank me, Amari, for my treetop adventure!" He grinned mischievously.

"Why?" she asked.

"I saw Besa walking through the forest, heading this way! I have seen how you tremble like a dove when he is near."

"You are the one who will be trembling if you do not get that coconut to Mother right away! And take her a few papayas and a pineapple as well. It will please her, and we shall have a delicious treat tonight." Amari could still smell the sweetness of the pineapple her mother had cut from its rough skin and sliced for the breakfast meal that morning.

Kwasi snatched back the coconut and ran off then, laughing and making kissing noises as he chanted, "Besa my love, Besa my love, Besa my love!" Amari pretended to chase him, but as soon as he was out of sight, she reached down into the small stream that flowed near Kwasi's tree and splashed water on her face.

Her village, Ziavi, lay just beyond the red dirt path down which Kwasi had disappeared. She headed there, walking leisurely, with just the slightest awareness of a certain new roundness to her hips and smoothness to her gait as she waited for Besa to catch up with her.

Amari loved the rusty brown dirt of Ziavi. The path, hard-packed from thousands of bare feet that had trod on it for decades, was flanked on both sides by fat, fruit-laden mango trees, the sweet smell of which always seemed to welcome her home. Ahead she could see the thatched roofs of the homes of her people, smoky cooking fires, and a chicken or two, scratching in the dirt.

She chuckled as she watched Tirza, a young woman about her own age, chasing one of her family's goats once again. That goat hated to be milked and always found a way to run off right at milking time. Tirza's mother had threatened several times to make stew of the hardheaded animal. Tirza waved at Amari, then dove after the goat, who had galloped into the undergrowth. Several of the old women, sitting in front of their huts soaking up sunshine, cackled with amusement.

To the left and apart from the other shelters in the village stood the home of the chief elder. It was larger than most, made of sturdy wood and bamboo, with thick thatch made from palm leaves making up the roof. The chief elder's two wives chattered cheerfully together as they pounded cassava fufu for his evening meal. Amari called out to them as she passed and bowed with respect.

She knew that she and her mother would soon be preparing the fufu for their own meal. She looked forward to the task—they would take turns pounding the vegetable into a wooden bowl with a stick almost as tall as Amari. Most of the time they got into such a good rhythm that her mother started tapping her feet and doing little dance steps as they worked. That always made Amari laugh.

Although Amari knew Besa was approaching, she pretended not to see him until he touched her shoulder. She turned quickly and, acting surprised, called out his name. "Besa!" Just seeing his face made her grin. He was much taller than she was, and she had to stand on tiptoe to look into his face. He had an odd little birthmark on his cheek—right at the place where his face dimpled into a smile. She thought it looked a little like a pineapple, but it disappeared as he smiled widely at the sight of her. He took her small brown hands into his large ones, and she felt as delicate as one of the little birds that Kwasi liked to catch and release.

"My lovely Amari," he greeted her. "How goes your day?" His deep voice made her tremble.

"Better, now that you are here," she replied. Amari and Besa had been formally betrothed to each other last year. They would be allowed to marry in another year. For now they simply enjoyed the mystery and pleasure of stolen moments such as this.

"I cannot stay and talk with you right now," Besa told her. "I have seen strangers in the forest, and I must tell the council of elders right away."

Amari looked intently at his face and realized he was worried. "What tribe are they from?" she asked with concern.

"I do not think the Creator made a tribe such as these creatures. They have skin the color of goat's milk." Besa frowned and ran to find the chief.

As she watched Besa rush off, an uncomfortable feeling filled Amari. The sunny pleasantness of the afternoon had suddenly turned dark. She hurried home to tell her family what she had learned. Her mother and Esi, a recently married friend, sat on the ground, spinning cotton threads for yarn. Their fingers flew as they chatted together, the pale fibers stretching and uncurling into threads for what would become kente cloth. Amari loved her tribe's design of animal figures and bold shapes. Tomorrow the women would dye the yarn, and when it was ready, her father, a master weaver, would create the strips of treasured fabric on his loom. Amari never tired of watching the magical rhythm of movement and color. Amari's mother looked up at her daughter warmly.

"You should be helping us make this yarn, my daughter," her mother chided gently.

"I'm sorry, Mother, it's just that I'd so much rather weave like father. Spinning makes my fingertips hurt." Amari had often imagined new patterns for the cloth, and longed to join the men at the long looms, but girls were forbidden to do so.

Her mother looked aghast. "Be content with woman's work, child. It is enough."

"I will help you with the dyes tomorrow," Amari promised halfheartedly. She avoided her mother's look of mild disapproval. "Besides, I was helping Kwasi gather fruit," Amari said, changing the subject.

Kwasi, sitting in the dirt trying to catch a grasshopper, looked up and said with a smirk, "I think she was more interested in making love-dove faces with Besa than making yarn with you!" When Amari reached out to grab him, he darted out of her reach, giggling.

"Your sister, even though she avoids the work, is a skilled spinner and will be a skilled wife. She needs practice in learning both, my son," their mother said with a smile. "Now disappear into the dust for a moment!" Kwasi ran off then, laughing as he chased the grasshopper, his bare feet barely skimming the dusty ground.

Amari knew her mother could tell by just the tilt of her smile or a fraction of a frown how she was feeling. "And how goes it with young Besa?" her mother asked quietly.

"Besa said that a band of unusual-looking strangers are coming this way, Mother," Amari informed her. "He seemed uneasy and went to tell the village elders."

"We must welcome our guests, then, Amari. We would never judge people simply by how they looked—that would be uncivilized," her mother told her. "Let us prepare for a celebration." Esi picked up her basket of cotton and, with a quick wave, headed home to make her own preparations.

Amari knew her mother was right and began to help her make plans for the arrival of the guests. They pounded fufu, made garden egg stew from eggplant and dried fish, and gathered more bananas, mangoes, and papayas.

"Will we have a dance and celebration for the guests, Mother?" she asked hopefully. "And Father's storytelling?"

"Your father and the rest of the elders will decide, but I'm sure the visit of such strangers will be cause for much festivity." Amari smiled with anticipation, for her mother was known as one of the most talented dancers in the Ewe tribe. Her mother continued, "Your father loves to have tales to tell and new stories to gather—this night will provide both."

Amari and her mother scurried around their small dwelling, rolling up the sleeping mats and sweeping the dirt floor with a broom made of branches. Throughout the village, the pungent smells of goat stew and peanut soup, along with waves of papaya and honeysuckle that wafted through the air, made Amari feel hungry as well as excited. The air was fragrant with hope and possibility.

POWERFUL TEEN FICTION
by SHARON M. DRAPER
bestselling author of the award-winning Hazelwood High trilogy

ROMIETTE & JULIO
0-689-84209-0 (Simon Pulse)
0-689-82180-8 (Atheneum)

THE BATTLE OF JERICHO
A Coretta Scott King Honor Book
0-689-84233-3 (Simon Pulse)
0-689-84232-5 (Atheneum)

COPPER SUN
0-689-82181-6 (Atheneum)

Simon & Schuster Children's Publishing Division
www.SimonSaysTEEN.com